DAVID FOENKINOS is the author of novels which have been translated into more than forty languages. His novel *Charlotte* won both the Prix Renaudot and the Prix Goncourt des lycéens in 2014, and *The Mystery of Henri Pick* (2020) was a *Guardian* Book of the Summer. *The Martins* (2022) was an *Independent* Book of the Month.

MEGAN JONES is a translator. She lives in London.

SECOND BEST

DAVID FOENKINOS

TRANSLATED FROM THE FRENCH BY
MEGAN JONES

GALLIC BOOKS
LONDON

A Gallic Book

First published in France as *Numéro deux*
by Editions Gallimard, 2022
Copyright © Editions Gallimard, Paris, 2022

English translation copyright © Gallic Books, 2023
First published in Great Britain in 2023 by
Gallic Books, Hamilton House, Mabledon Place, London, WC1H 9BD

This paperback edition published 2024

A CIP record for this book is available from the British Library

ISBN 978-1-913547-74-5

Typeset in Garamond by Andy Barr

Printed and bound by LSI

NOTE TO THE READER

Although some aspects of this novel are based on real events, the author has sought to let his imagination run free in this entirely fictional tale.

In 1999 the search to find the young boy who would play Harry Potter began. The boy who would become world-famous. Hundreds of actors were auditioned. In the end, only two remained. This novel tells the story of the boy who wasn't chosen.

PART ONE

1

In order to understand the depth of Martin Hill's trauma, we must go back to where it all began. In 1999 he had just turned ten, and lived in London with his father. He remembered this period as happy. In a photo from that time he could be seen with a smile as wide as a promise. The preceding months, however, had been difficult; his mother had left them to return to Paris. By mutual agreement, and so as not to cut him off from his friends, adding another separation on top of *their* separation, it was decided that young Martin would remain with his father. He saw his mother every weekend and during the holidays. The Eurostar, though more often praised for bringing France and England together, also hugely eased logistics for separated families. To tell the truth, Martin was very little affected by the change. Like all children who grow up seeing their parents argue, he could no longer bear their permanent state of disagreement. Jeanne had ended up hating everything that she had once loved about John. Where she had once adored his artistic, dreamy side, now she saw nothing more than a lazy lump.

They had met at a Cure concert in 1984, at a time when John had the same haircut as the singer, a sort of baobab tree sprouting from his head. Jeanne was working as an au pair for a wealthy, yet strict, young English couple, and she wore her hair in a pristine bob. If compatibility were measured in haircuts, they never would have met. What is more, Jeanne had ended up at the concert somewhat by chance, persuaded by another French girl, Camille, whom she had met in Hyde Park. Both girls noticed this bizarre individual at the back of the room looking wasted. He was downing beer after beer while the band played song after song. After a while, his knees gave way. The two girls went over to him to help him back on his feet; he tried to thank them, but his furry tongue was beyond producing any intelligible sound. They took him to the exit so he could get some air. John was just lucid enough to feel sorry for himself. Camille, a devoted fan, returned to the concert, while Jeanne stayed beside the troubled young man. Later she would ask herself: Should I have fled? The moment we met he was already falling apart. That's not nothing. 'Mistrust first impulses; they are nearly always good,' as Henry de Montherlant wrote. Or at least, Jeanne thought it was he who had written it, most likely in *The Girls*, a book that all her friends had been devouring at the time. Years later, she would discover that the quote was in fact by Talleyrand. In any case, Jeanne let herself be won over by the boy's strangeness. It bears mentioning that he had a particular – perhaps what one would call British – sense of humour. As he regained his wits, he said, falteringly: 'I've always dreamed of being at the back of a rock concert downing beers. I've always dreamed of being that cool guy. But nothing doing. I'm just a loser who loves Schweppes and Schubert.'

So Jeanne missed the incredible eight-minute version of 'A Forest': Robert Smith loved to draw out this trippy song which had been their first hit in the British charts. It started to rain heavily, and the two of them took refuge in a taxi heading for the centre of London, where John lived in a tiny flat he had inherited from his grandmother. Before she died, she had told him: 'I'll leave you the flat on one condition: that you water the flowers on my grave once a week.' The honouring of an open-ended contract between the living and the dead is admittedly somewhat unusual – but perhaps this was another example of British humour. Anyway, the deal was done, and the grandson never broke his promise. But let's return to the living: that night Jeanne decided to go up to John's flat, which was quite unlike her. They deemed it sensible to undress, so as not to stay in their soaking-wet clothes. Once they were naked, facing one another, they had no choice but to have sex.

Early next morning John suggested they go to the cemetery – he had to pay his dues. Jeanne thought this idea for their first walk utterly charming. They strolled for hours, in the first throes of love. Neither of them imagined that, fifteen years later, it would all come crashing down.

2

They loved that their names were John and Jeanne. They spent hours telling each other stories, all the pages of their pasts. At the start of a relationship, the beloved is a Russian novel: long, deep and wild. They discovered they had a lot in common. Literature, for example. They both loved Nabokov and vowed one day to go butterfly-catching in his honour. At that time, Margaret Thatcher was brutally ignoring the demands and stifling the hopes of the striking miners. Neither of them cared. Happiness doesn't trouble itself with the conditions of the working class. Happiness is always a little bourgeois.

John was at art college, but his true passion was inventing. His latest creation was the umbrella-tie, an object that would surely become indispensable for every British person. Though the idea was brilliant, it had nonetheless hit a wall of general disinterest. Clock-pens were still all the rage. Jeanne told him over and over that all geniuses experienced rejection to begin with. He had to give the world time to catch up with his talent, she added loftily and with affection. For her part, Jeanne had fled to London to escape her parents, who had never known how to express their love. She already spoke perfect English. She dreamed of becoming a political journalist, interviewing heads of state – although she didn't really know where this obsession had come from. Eight years later, she would put a question to François Mitterrand at a press conference in Paris. In her eyes, this would mark the start of her success. First, she quit her job as a nanny to become a waitress in a restaurant whose speciality was an excellent chilli. She quickly worked out that she had only to speak with a strong French accent to earn bigger tips. Day after day, she perfected the art of riddling her English with mistakes. She liked it when John watched her from the street, waiting for the end of her shift. Then, when she finally left work, they would walk through the night. She would tell him about some rude customers she'd had, and he would enthusiastically explain his latest idea to her. Between them, there was a harmony that was part dream, part reality.

After several months of hoarding her tips, Jeanne decided she had saved up enough to leave her job. She wrote a magnificent covering letter which landed her an internship with *The Guardian*. As she was French, they asked her to assist the newspaper's Paris correspondent. This was a blow. She had hoped for an exciting life, running around reporting here and there, but her role consisted of organising meetings and booking train tickets. It was ironic, but being a waitress had felt more intellectually stimulating. Luckily, the situation improved. Through sheer determination she showed what she was capable of, and was soon given more responsibility. She even published her first article. In a couple of lines, she described the advent of soup kitchens in France. John read and re-read these few words as though it was a sacred text. It was an incredible feeling, seeing the name of the woman he loved in the newspaper – or rather, her initials, J. G. (Her last name was Godard, though no relation to the French-Swiss director.)

When she arrived at the office a few days later, she discovered among the classified ads these three lines, written in French

INVENTOR WITHOUT A BRIGHT IDEA

HAS SEEN THE LIGHT.

WILL YOU MARRY ME J.G.?

Jeanne sat stunned at her desk for several minutes. Such happiness startled her. For a moment, she thought: I'll pay for this one day. But her mind quickly returned to the idyllic direction her life was going in. She briefly tried to think of an original response, a 'yes' that would surprise him, something spectacular that would match his proposal. On the other hand, no. She picked up the telephone, dialled their home number, and when he answered she simply said: yes. The ceremony was intimate and rainy. At the town hall, a song by the Cure played as the bride and groom entered. The few invited friends applauded the couple who, as is traditional, kissed passionately after exchanging their vows. Unfortunately, and rather surprisingly, no one had thought to bring a camera. Perhaps it was better that way. Without physical traces of happiness, there is less chance of eventually drowning in nostalgia.

They then went away for a few days to a little farm in the heart of the English countryside, and spent their honeymoon learning how to milk cows. Upon their return, they moved into a larger two-bedroom flat. This place would allow them each to have some space if ever they argued, they said to each other, smiling. It was that wonderful time in a relationship when humour comes so readily; everything is so easy to laugh at. But this didn't stop Jeanne from having big plans for her career. Even if she thought her husband was gifted, it didn't mean she was prepared to take financial responsibility for both of them. He had to grow up, he had to work. Why must we always submit to the practical side of life? John wondered. But thankfully, things fell easily into place. Stuart, an old friend from art college who was now a film production designer, invited John to join his team. So John found himself on the set of *A View to a Kill*, the new James Bond film. Among his contributions was the green paint on a door handle opened by Roger Moore. For years, every time the film was on, he would shout, 'That's my door handle!' as though the success of the entire film relied on that prop. He took pleasure in being part of the silent army that hurried about behind the scenes. And so the years passed, alternating between film shoots and fruitless attempts at inventing something revolutionary.

On the night of the New Year's Eve that would see 1988 turn into 1989, Jeanne was overcome with nausea, though she hadn't yet had a drink. She sensed immediately that she was pregnant. At the stroke of midnight, while they were in the middle of a party and everyone was kissing each other, she said to John, not 'Happy New Year, my love,' but instead, 'Happy New Year, Papa.' It took him a few seconds to understand, and then he almost fainted – he had a melodramatic streak. Quite understandably, though: he, who was lost in a desert, devoid of inspiration, was going to create a human being. And so Martin was born, on 23 June 1989, at Queen Charlotte's and Chelsea Hospital, one of the oldest maternity hospitals in Europe. The new parents had chosen his name because it was easily understood on both sides of the Channel. In fact, without getting ahead of ourselves, it was in that same hospital, exactly one month later, that Daniel Radcliffe – the actor who would go on to play Harry Potter – first entered the world.

3

Martin's arrival, naturally, changed their life. The lightness of their early days was over; now they had to do sums, predict, anticipate. All this planning was incompatible with John's nature. He was still working on films, but not enough. Several production designers no longer wanted to work with him, finding him too fiery whenever disagreements arose over artistic choices. Jeanne had tried to teach him diplomacy, or at least how to choose his words more carefully, but he clearly had a problem with authority. He often spent his time criticising those in power. During these rages, he even denigrated the newspaper his wife worked for, claiming it was in thrall to those in power.[1] And yet *The Guardian* was hardly known for being lenient towards the government. In these moments, Jeanne couldn't bear his constant complaining, this attitude that revealed his bitterness. She would feel so aggravated by him – but then her tender feelings would come back.

John was an amateur genius. Should he have been angry at himself for not being blessed with inspiration? Can you die of not being Mozart, when all you can get out of the piano are second-rate melodies? He basked in the role of misunderstood artist. He was the sort who wanted to slum it at rock concerts despite hating the music. Perhaps his entire personality could be summed up in this central contradiction: John dreamed of being an inventor, but he had no real ideas. He suffered from an unfulfilled creative force that he felt in the deepest part of him. Luckily, fatherhood offered him a way to nurture his

---

1 A few years later, Jeanne was walking through a bookshop and couldn't stop herself from buying the new Philip Roth novel, *I Married a Communist*.

creativity: he loved making up all manner of games. Martin was incredibly proud to have a father like him. Their daily life was full of surprises; each day held something new. In his son's eyes, John could do no wrong. And the way his son gazed at him helped John to calm down, gradually alleviating his frustrations.

On a professional level, things began to improve as well. On set one day, he had to stand in for a prop designer who was unwell. It was like an epiphany. It was a complicated job that required quick decision-making. His role consisted in sorting out the practical problems: placing a wedge under a chair that had suddenly become wobbly, finding a corkscrew that was easier to operate, or changing the colour of a teabag. Not only was John more autonomous in this job, but he also thrived under the constant pressure. He had found a vocation that mixed inventiveness with design – everyone has a calling. In his words, he had become a 'last-minute artist'.

4

Jeanne hadn't suffered the same difficulties. Her star was in the ascendant. She had managed to realise her dream of joining the politics team, and often travelled with her work, as a roving reporter. When she phoned her son from these business trips, he coloured in her location on a map. There came a time when his mother's footsteps covered a large part of Europe. Without realising it, Jeanne had begun to distance herself from her home. John became like one of those first loves that don't survive into adulthood. It was evident that they had grown apart. But so many couples survive despite being incompatible. There were so many reasons still to love one another: their son, their past, the embers of their passion. Jeanne was fond of John, but did she still love him? She wanted to preserve their love story, but as time went on, she felt something essential was passing her by; her heart was beating in a way that was far too sensible. She was sometimes annoyed by their domestic quarrels: you didn't put this away, why did you forget that. These household disputes drove her up the wall. She'd had higher hopes for her life. But these reproaches were a way of expressing her frustration.

Some stories are written even before they begin. Jeanne got on well with one of her colleagues in the sport section. They had lunch together a few times, in that seemingly innocent way that masks the ambush of seduction. Then he suggested: 'Why don't we go for a drink one evening?' She had said yes without thinking. The strangest part was that she didn't tell her husband the truth; she gave the excuse of the newspaper going to press late. It was all there, in that lie which betrayed what she was truly feeling. After the drink, there was the suggestion of dinner – which required another lie – then a second dinner, then a kiss, and then the idea of finding a hotel. Jeanne acted surprised, but her reaction was nothing more than a façade, concealing her elation. She desired this man; she thought about him constantly, about his face, his body. Sensuality returned to the foreground of her life. And he felt the same way; he had never cheated on his wife before. Beneath his self-assured manner lay an intense turmoil. Ashamed and surprised at themselves in equal measure, they swore their affair would not last long. They just wanted to inject some passion into their everyday existence, and tried to do so without being crushed by guilt. Life was too short to be perfect.

But then the deceived wife interrupted this little interlude when she came across their messages. She could have left her husband, but instead demanded an immediate end to the affair. He complied at once, not wanting to give up the family he had created or his life with his three children. He resigned from the newspaper and found a position with a local television channel in Manchester, for which he had to move house. Jeanne never saw him again. She remained in a daze for weeks, frightened by how quickly her happiness had vanished. Going to work became painful. She realised that this affair, which she had believed to be something casual, had shaken her to the core. Affairs of the heart being ever ironic, John had been particularly loving throughout that period. The more Jeanne seemed to pull away, the closer he tried to get to her. But he was a nuisance; she needed to be alone. She didn't love him any more. She started arguments over nothing. She embraced falling out of love.

Suddenly, Jeanne could no longer stand England, that land filled with the visible reminders of her aborted passion. But what could she do? Martin was only nine years old. She was trapped. She couldn't uproot him by returning to France, even less take him away from his father. Then fate decided for her. She was offered a job as a political journalist for *L'Événement du jeudi*. Georges-Marc Benamou had just taken over the weekly newspaper and was eager to rejuvenate and energise it. She had met him in London when Tony Blair was elected. They had certainly got along, but she never imagined he would call on her. Jeanne felt this was surely a sign, a hand reaching out towards her future. Just before they went to sleep, in the darkness of the bedroom, she told her husband softly: 'I'm leaving.' John turned on the light and asked her where on earth she thought she was going at this late hour.

She talked about their last few years together. In this sudden urge to confess, she was unsure whether or not to reveal her infidelity, but decided against it. There was nothing to be gained by causing even more damage now that it was over. She spoke of feeling worn down, of how time was passing – generic phrases that said everything and nothing all at once. And then she brought up the professional opportunity she had been offered.

Three times, John sighed: 'It can't be, it can't be, it can't be,' until eventually he said: 'You can still go to Paris if it's important to you. I'll take care of everything. And we can see each other every weekend.'

'That's not what I want. I want to move forward.'

'. . .'

'It's over between us.'

'. . .'

'I'm so sorry.'

'. . .'

'Martin can stay with you. I don't want to cut him off from his life here, from his friends. He can come and stay with me at the weekends, and during holidays... That is, if you agree...'

John was silent. It wasn't a discussion; it was a statement. He began to imagine himself alone in the flat, his son on the other side of the Channel. Soon she would ask for full custody, he was sure of it. At the start she would try to cajole him, pushing him little by little towards losing his son.

What would become of him? How would he live without her? He let his mind wallow in the darkest vision of his future.

5

A new life began. John tried not to show what he was feeling – that he was a clown in the circus of separation. When he took Martin to the station on Friday evenings, he grinned and said, without fail, 'Kiss the Eiffel Tower for me!' Any child would have been able to detect the pathos in this joke. For every journey, he made Martin a tuna mayonnaise sandwich which he wrapped carefully in tinfoil, a ritual that was a pure demonstration of love. Then he returned home where the solitude was deafening. He spent most of his weekends imagining the walks his son was taking with Jeanne. Where were they going? What were they doing? But when he picked Martin up from the station on Sunday nights, he hardly asked him any questions. He didn't have the strength to hear tales of their life without him. Instead, he just asked his son: 'So, was the sandwich good?'

6

It was 1999. Martin was a young English boy like any other. A football-crazy Arsenal fan, he had jumped for joy when Nicolas Anelka joined his favourite team. When Anelka scored a goal, Martin was proud to have a French mother. What else is there to tell? His favourite singer was Michael Jackson. He had a poster of Princess Diana in his bedroom. He dreamed of one day owning a dog he would name Jack. Also worth mentioning is the crush he had on Betty, a redhead who preferred his friend Matthew to him. But some days, he wasn't sure that he really liked her. He found her loudmouthed ways insufferable. Perhaps he was looking for flaws to ease the pain of rejection. At ten years old, he already understood that one of the ways of being happy was to change your perception of reality. The same reality that you can escape with flights of imagination, or the images conjured when reading books. All around him, people were talking more and more about a book called *Harry Potter*. His friend Lucy swore by the story of the wizard. But Martin felt no particular desire to follow the crowd. The books he had to read for school were more than enough for him. In general, he felt no real artistic calling. He didn't want to learn a musical instrument, nor did he feel comfortable on stage during the end-of-year plays. The few times his father had taken him to a film set, he had been profoundly bored. Naturally – a child on a James Ivory set is like a vegetarian in a butcher's shop.

Martin's life might have continued like this. Nothing that happened subsequently was preordained. For him to end up at the *Harry Potter* audition, there had to be a change of trajectory. Which is exactly what happened – twice.

Fate is always thought to be a positive force, propelling us towards a magical future. Surprisingly, its negative side is very rarely mentioned, as though fate has entrusted the management of its brand image to a PR genius. We always say, for example, 'As luck would have it!' Which entirely obscures the idea that the things that luck would have are not always lucky.

Firstly, there was a long lorry drivers' strike in Britain in the spring of 1999. They were fighting for an improvement in their working conditions. For weeks, London was cut off from the rest of the country with no supplies, without even essential foodstuffs. But that will play its part a little later on. For the moment, Martin is at school. Every year, the students had to have a medical examination, a basic evaluation of their well-being. The children were always delighted at the chance to miss an hour of lessons. Just like during fire drills, when a torturous science class was replaced by joyful roaming. Therefore, peeing into a jar became a joy. Martin wasn't sporty – he could even be considered rather puny – but he stood up straight and looked energetic. The nurse who was examining him took his blood pressure, made him take a deep breath and then cough, and tapped his knees with a strange hammer to test his reflexes. Finally, she asked him to stand up and touch his toes. Then she asked him a few questions about his family life and his diet, a sort of fast-track psychoanalysis in which Martin announced his mother had left to live in France while also admitting that he never ate broccoli.

Finally there was an eye test which is still fun as an adult. There is something exciting about trying to make out that Lilliputian alphabet. You squint your eyes in an exaggerated, ridiculous manner, and end up seeing an H instead of an M. In Martin's case, the verdict was damning. 'Your eyesight has deteriorated since last year. You're going to have to wear glasses,' the nurse decreed. At ten years old, this is pretty good news. You don't yet know about the hours you will waste looking everywhere for those two round pieces of glass that you cannot leave the house without; nor do you know that you will break them before an important meeting and have to muddle through in a complete fog. And you don't know that if one day you have to wear a surgical mask, you will go about the world at the mercy of misted-up lenses. For now, Martin thinks that glasses will give him a serious air, or at least an intelligent one – one that Betty might like.

That evening, Martin relayed the news to his father, who couldn't help feeling that this was a consequence of the separation. 'His eyesight is getting worse because he doesn't want to see the new reality of his life.' An interesting theory, but not one that would change the course of events. Jeanne wasn't going to suddenly return to London because her son had lost a tenth of the vision in his left eye. The next day, they went to the optician. Strangely, there wasn't a single pair of glasses on the display stands.

'I can't stock up until the strike is over. I barely have anything,' the optician's assistant explained.

'So what can we do?' asked John.

'You'd have to ask the lorry drivers that. I'll show you the catalogue, and your son can choose the style he wants. I'll order them as soon as I can.'

'. . .'

'In the meantime, I can offer you these ones here.'

The man opened a drawer and took out a pair of round glasses with black frames. Martin, rather miffed, looked at them. When he tried them on, he found his face looked a little strange. The optician added that he could put in the correct lenses that same day.

'They really suit you! We don't even need to look at the catalogue. Really, they're perfect!' John gushed. Martin was immediately convinced that this enthusiasm was fake and had only one aim: to avoid having to come back here.

And that's how Martin came to wear round glasses.

7

The second agent of fate was named Rose Hampton, a young woman of twenty-two who looked after Martin while his father was on set. Martin was fascinated by her ever-changing hair

– she was forever dying it different colours. A few years later, when he discovered the film *Eternal Sunshine of the Spotless Mind*, Kate Winslet's character immediately made him think of Rose. She had the same charisma, the same sweet zaniness. Martin would never have dared admit it for fear of seeming ridiculous, but he had feelings for her. Sometimes, in the body of a child beats the heart of a man. Unfortunately, she was in a relationship with a cricket-playing moron. But that wasn't the important thing. The important thing was a fall down the stairs.

Margaret, Rose's beloved grandmother, had missed a step on the staircase and taken a violent tumble. She died instantly. Devastated, the young woman left straight away for Brighton to organise the funeral, and to let herself be overcome by an immeasurable grief. She wandered along the seashore for days on end, haunted by happy memories from her childhood. It was absurd that her grandmother should die like that, when old age didn't seem to have taken hold of her yet. One wrong step, off by perhaps a millimetre, had been deadly. One tiny mistake could push you towards death. And it was this same infinitesimal misstep, this sprinkling of misfortune, that would dramatically change Martin's destiny too. The step missed by his babysitter's grandmother would be the root cause of his tragedy.

Rose threw some things into a suitcase without really thinking of what season it was, and hurried to Victoria Station. Just before getting on the train, she had an epiphany: she couldn't just vanish without telling anyone. She phoned her boyfriend and then her best friend, before dialling one final number. She left a garbled message on the answer machine, saying she wouldn't be able to look after Martin the next day. That evening, when he listened to the message, John was irritated. He wondered what could possibly have happened to Rose for her to disappear so suddenly – she hadn't given any details – and then his thoughts moved straight on to another question: who would look after Martin?

John had accepted the job of back-up prop designer on a film that was already being touted as a success, *Notting Hill*. Everyone was raving about the pairing of Hugh Grant and Julia Roberts. John was involved mainly in the scenes filmed outside on Portobello Road, where he had to recreate authentic shopfronts with great precision. Stuart Craig, the production designer, had done a wonderful job. With his background in costume dramas, he was very taken with the idea of a project where realism was crucially important to the blossoming of the love story. Unable to find a replacement for Rose, John had no choice but to take his son with him. Martin was used to sets, and to sitting quietly in a corner. In any case, as a precaution John had warned the head of production that he would bring his son with him the next day. The head of production replied that it was good timing: Martin could be an extra.

The stage was set.

Before continuing, we must take a quick trip back in time, to the story of a writer who today is known around the world.

The fairy-tale story of J. K. Rowling is well known. Imagine a young woman, living an unstable existence and bringing up her child on her own, who suddenly becomes the greatest heroine in British history. It's a story which seems plucked from the mind of a scriptwriter with a great sense of humour. The tale begins on 31 July 1965, in Yate, a town in the middle of

England. Joanne's love of reading had been instilled in her from an early age by her mother, so much so that she recalls having written her first story at the age of six. Certainly, we can cast doubt on much that has been said about her. The more famous someone is, the more everyone seems to have an opinion about their past. Everyone you've ever met is ready to share their memory of you, whether a scandalous revelation or a happy anecdote; the most insignificant person, who once handed you a bowl of crisps at a party, might decide to write an essay on you.

At any rate, the one thing everyone agrees on is Joanne's impressive imagination as a young girl. But it's a well-known fact that a talent for writing never equates to happiness. An introvert, Joanne describes her teenage self as quiet, short-sighted and covered in freckles. In short, all the misfortune necessary to shape a future artist. It was then the young girl learned that her mother had multiple sclerosis, a progressive degenerative disease – a terrible countdown to death. It was a huge shock. As a tribute, Joanne decided to follow in her mother's footsteps as a teacher. During her studies, she spent several months in Paris, where she lived close to a bookshop that no longer exists today. In the end, she landed a job as a secretary, with a responsibility for translations, at Amnesty International. There she would find herself confronted with suffering that would haunt her. Much later, she said she began to have 'literal nightmares about some of the things I saw, heard and read'. Here and there, among these biographical titbits, we can see the genesis of her fictional universe.

We find her next in the Chamber of Commerce in Manchester. It's difficult to imagine a bleaker existence, but boredom remains the best training ground for a writer. More and more often, Joanne would escape into her imagination (the literary version of daydreaming), until the day in 1990 when, on a train from Manchester to London, she was struck by inspiration.[2]

With her forehead pressed to the window, and no paper or pencil to write down her ideas, the story of Harry Potter took shape in her mind. She explained that everything emerged at once: the general outline of all seven books. But following this dazzling stroke of inspiration, she suffered a major blow when her mother died six months later.

Finally, a new world was opening up to her. Through an advertisement published in *The Guardian*, she got a job as an English teacher in Portugal. There she met Jorge, a journalist, with whom she had a daughter, Jessica. But their relationship was tumultuous, and in the end he hit her, chasing her through the streets of Porto in the middle of the night. In recent interviews, he admits to having slapped her, but denies mistreatment – a rather difficult paradox to understand. So Joanne returned to the UK with her daughter, without the slightest prospect, professional or personal. First staying with her sister in Edinburgh, she soon found a small apartment, and survived on benefits. The fairy tale was running on empty. She judged her life a disaster, and fell into a depression. She would later explain that these dark hours inspired the creation of Dementors, those faceless, evil creatures who suck the joy and happy memories out of their victims. Eventually she found a job and began teaching again. Whenever she could steal an hour, she wrote with a fury that could be described as the energy of hopelessness. Little by little, the pages stacked up. The story was taking shape.

In 1995, her manuscript completed, she went into a bookshop

---

2   It is said that all writers lacking in inspiration take the same train, in the hope of being struck by a miracle themselves.

in Edinburgh where she came across a list of literary agents. She was drawn to the name Christopher Little, and decided to send the sheaf of papers to his agency's office, in Fulham, southwest London. His assistant, Bryony Evans, fell under the spell of the story, and encouraged her boss to read it. The first few chapters were enough to convince him, and he telephoned the author. Joanne couldn't believe it. She wanted to shout for joy, but the agent's words rang in her head: 'Nothing is certain yet.' The following months would confirm this. The first twelve publishers he contacted rejected the manuscript categorically. A year went by, and then Little learned that Bloomsbury was creating a children's list. He decided to address the manuscript to Barry Cunningham, who was immediately taken with the book's opening. But Joanne's fortunes were ultimately in the hands of an eight-year-old girl, Alice Newton. The managing director, in search of a child's opinion, had his daughter read the first chapter of *Harry Potter*. She was enthralled by it, and immediately wanted to read the next. It was this enthusiasm that sparked the greatest publishing craze the world has ever seen.

The contract was signed. The editor advised Joanne to change her first name so that the book, written as it was by a woman, would not be pigeonholed as a 'book for girls'. And so she became 'J. K.' on the cover of this first volume, which was published on 26 June 1997. The K stood for Kathleen, the name of her paternal grandmother. The first print run was modest, just 2,500 copies, but they soon had to reprint many times over. A few weeks later, the book sat squarely at the top of the bestseller lists, and it was already being dubbed a phenomenon. While Joanne wrote the next book, the sensation continued. The book was translated throughout the world after a significant bidding war. Just one element was missing to put the finishing touches to the miracle: a film adaptation

9

Because of who his parents were, David Heyman had grown up in the world of cinema. Among other things, his mother Norma had produced Stephen Frears's *Dangerous Liaisons*, and John, his father, had been one of the financial backers of masterworks such as *Marathon Man* and *Chinatown*. One can only imagine the pressure weighing on the young man's shoulders when he threw himself into the profession too. At every meeting he must have heard, 'Ah! I knew your father well!' or 'How is your mother?' All the 'sons of' and 'daughters of' are surely familiar with constantly being reminded of their place in the family hierarchy. David could have chosen another occupation, where he would have been shielded from comparisons, but no – cinema was his calling. He decided to move to the USA, where he built a respectable career, moving from United Artists to Warner Bros. But at thirty-five years old, homesickness and a desire to be close to his family and friends again pushed him to return to London and set up his own company. Heyday Films was created in 1996.

The new desks and state-of-the-art photocopier awaited their projects. When it came to hiring an assistant, David's father insisted that he should help one of his old colleagues, who had been out of work for a long time. Ann Taylor barely spoke during the interview, and wasn't much of a film buff. The last film she had seen at the cinema was *Out of Africa* in 1985. But David wanted to please his father, especially since John had told him, 'You know, life hasn't treated Ann too kindly.' Ann's hardships had indeed affected her self-esteem, to the point where she considered solitude the best place in which to take refuge.

The young producer spent his days reading the scripts he had received, but nothing piqued his interest. Sometimes his parents would come and have lunch with him, and David briefly mentioned some projects, but they could tell it was best to talk about something else. On top of that, it rained all the time. David, who had thought he could no longer stand Los Angeles, began to miss his night-time walks along Venice Beach. Had he made a mistake in coming back to London?

Every Monday morning he had a meeting with external collaborators, in which Ann took notes of everything that was said. David wanted to specialise in book adaptations, so each person arrived with a list of books they felt could be turned into films. A few days earlier, a parcel had arrived at the office, sent by Christopher Little. It contained *Harry Potter and the Philosopher's Stone*, a children's novel that hadn't yet been published. Due, surely, to its colourful cover, Ann decided to take it home for the weekend. Caught up in the story of the boy who had enrolled in a wizarding school, she decided to bring it up at the meeting. But her shyness stopped her. All day, she'd wanted to go in to talk to David. Although she had prepared and practised the words she would say, she was afraid of sounding silly. But she tried to banish her apprehension, carried along by the conviction that she needed to share her enthusiasm for this book. For years, she had lived cut off from the world. Reading this book had propelled her into a kind of joyous, magical kingdom. She thought that if this book had done her some good, then other people might be similarly touched by it. Finally, she gathered her courage (and the book) and headed for David's office. Suddenly her fear stopped her once more, and she froze. At that precise moment, her boss came out of his office and found her standing motionless outside the door.

'Is something wrong?'

'Sorry, no. Everything is fine. It's just that . . . this morning, I forgot to talk to you about this book,' she stammered, holding out the novel.

She could have left it at that, but she wanted to tell him a bit about the story. At first glance, the concept didn't interest David at all. It wasn't the type of film he wanted to produce. He dreamed instead of a psychological drama that would win him an Oscar. There was talk of a thought-provoking project that Stanley Kubrick would soon be filming in London, one that would reunite the most glamorous couple in the world: Tom Cruise and Nicole Kidman. That was what he was looking for, and Ann was talking about an orphan flying around on a broomstick. Really, it was nonsense. Then Ann began to cough. The woman's fragility completed disarmed him. If she hadn't coughed, everything might have been different. So he took the book, out of politeness – or pity, perhaps – thanked her, and put it in his bag.

10

For the next few days, nothing happened. David must have forgotten about his secretary's recommendation. In the meantime, she had reread the book, to confirm her first impression. Struck by the same feeling, at the end of the meeting the following Monday she dared to ask, 'So, have you read it?' To David's ears, it sounded like a reminder from his financial advisor. No, he hadn't had the time, he said, which was completely untrue. In actual fact, he'd had no desire whatsoever to immerse himself in this story, but at that exact moment he thought again of his father's words: 'You know, life hasn't treated Ann too kindly . . .' He could at least skim through the story, skip a few pages. So he promised to read it, and did so that evening. Comfortably installed in his armchair, he opened the novel and read the first sentence. And then the second.

All at once, the sentences joined together in a sharp, joyful style. Like millions of readers were also to discover, David found the novel to be a surprising breath of fresh air. He had planned to watch a television programme later that evening, but the desire vanished without him even realising. He allowed the story to absorb him. He couldn't stop turning the pages. How long had it been since he had felt that way? He couldn't remember. Perhaps since he'd read Paul Auster's *Moon Palace*, and that was only because he was having dinner with the author after the preview of his film *Smoke* in New York. In the end, the meeting never happened; the writer-director had abandoned all his social obligations that evening. But to return to *Harry Potter*, it had been a long time since David had taken such pleasure in reading. It is very difficult now to imagine reading this book back when no one had heard of it, unaware of all the commentary about it, knowing nothing of the phenomenon that it was to become. To do so is to try and imagine reading *Harry Potter* before the success of *Harry Potter*. Only a handful of readers, David among them, had this unique experience, only possible nowadays for an alien. So at that moment, before the first book had even been released, it wasn't at all clear that the story would make a good film.

However, that was David's first thought, and this was the essence of his talent as a producer. He could already picture the Dursleys' house and Hogwarts School. Of course, it would be expensive, but he could speak to his old partners at Warner Bros. The only problem was that no one knew the book, and it was preferable, particularly for a film that would need a large budget, to adapt a story that had already gathered a wide audience. His mind was racing, but wasn't he getting ahead of himself? And what if the rights weren't available? First and foremost, he needed to meet the author. Who was hiding behind the initials J. K.?

11

The next morning, after a sleepless night, David entered Ann's office. Looking at his pale face, she thought he must have been out in Soho until the early hours. But he instantly disabused her of that idea when he began to enthuse about the book. She thought initially that he was just being polite, because she had insisted he read the book – but no. He began describing the plot, and the multitude of details he mentioned left no doubt in her mind: he had devoured the book. Ann felt a profound joy, a disproportionate joy, perhaps; after all, she had simply recommended a book to her superior, and he was finally sharing his opinion with her. But something else made her happy: the idea that she could be trusted, that she had good instincts. In other words, that she could be counted on. Knowing the rest of the story, it's likely that this eased her self-doubt and put an end to her constant questioning of her own worth.

'Do you know who the author is?' asked David.

'Yes, I found out. She's a thirty-two-year-old woman.'

'A woman? I thought it was a man . . . I don't know why.'

'I imagine that was the point of using the initials J. K. – to sow confusion.'

'Ah, perhaps . . .'

'There's no further information about her on the proofs. Just that Little is managing her.'

'Very good. Call him and set up a meeting.'

'Of course, I'll take care of it,' she replied. A few minutes later she went into David's office. 'As it happens, Bloomsbury are organising a small cocktail party for the book launch. It's this evening, and the author will be there.'

'. . .'

'And you're invited.'

She said these last words in a monotone, as though everything was normal. They hung in the air meaningfully. David would attend the cocktail party, and he would meet J. K. Rowling. He asked Ann to accompany him; after all, it had been she who had discovered the book. She thought about it for a moment, then declined the invitation. She gave an excuse – she had to feed Chekhov and Tolstoy, her two cats – yes, that was it. Ann thought it very gracious of David to invite her, but she felt uncomfortable at these types of parties, where you had to simultaneously smile idiotically while also saying intelligent things. She did, however, relish the idea of being a kind of silent partner. That evening, on the packed Tube train, no one could have imagined that this commuter was about to make her mark on cinematic history as the instigator of a worldwide phenomenon.

12

David felt a pressure building up inside him as he arrived at the party. After giving his name and his coat to the doorman, he headed to the bar in search of a glass of water. His mouth was dry. Drinking it down in one, his eyes swept the room. What did she look like, this author he had come to meet? A young woman approached him.

'David! What are you doing here?' He didn't immediately recognise who was speaking to him, surely due to the turmoil he was feeling. But he knew perfectly well how to handle the situation. He just had to let the conversation glide along at surface level before he could pluck from mid-air the piece of crucial information that would allow him to identify the speaker. It was Emily, a classmate from university. These days she worked at Bloomsbury. It's always best to know someone, David thought at once.

'I've come to meet the author,' he said eventually, adding self-consciously, 'to ask her about a possible film project.' Emily offered to make the introductions, but she could no longer see Joanne anywhere in the room. She must have gone outside for some air. Emily took the opportunity to fill the gap in the conversation before it could set in.

'We don't usually throw book launches for small print runs like this. We invited some journalists from children's magazines, and some librarians who are organising *Harry Potter* competitions.' After a few more statements like this, Joanne appeared at last. Emily and David moved towards her. In a film, this scene would have been in slow motion. But in a book . . . it's difficult . . . to slow down . . . the pace of . . . the action . . . unless you use . . . ellipses . . .

'Is everything okay?' Emily asked, concerned by Joanne's pale face.

'Yes, everything's fine. I just popped out for a moment. It's overwhelming.'

'I understand. Allow me to introduce David. He's a friend of mine who produces films, and he would like to speak to you.'

'Oh . . . good evening.'

'Good evening. I'm very happy to meet you, especially after

having spent hours with your characters. I was spellbound by your book.'

'Could we sit down?' said Joanne, as though it were impossible for her to accept this compliment while standing up.

Emily slipped away, thinking it best to leave them to talk. They went up to a seat, and Joanne sat down immediately. David said haltingly that if this wasn't a good time, they could talk later, but she insisted he stay. She admitted she felt rather out of her depth among all these people who had come here for her. She wasn't used to this sort of organised fun. Little could she have imagined that, soon, her entire world would resemble this cocktail party.

While David resumed discussion of her book, Joanne lowered her head. It seemed odd that he was describing her work, as though a stranger was repeating back to her something she had confided to her therapist. Joanne listened to him recounting the goings-on at Hogwarts in minute detail. Carried away by his enthusiasm, he began to talk of the film he already had in mind. This time, she interrupted him.

'A film? Really?'

'Yes, a film.'

'Look, it's very touching, what you've said,' Joanne began. 'You can't imagine how touching. But you're going too far now.'

'. . .'

'You're a friend of Emily's, and you want me to have a nice evening. And I am having a nice evening, in fact. But don't talk to me about a film. Who am I to dream of that? The book hasn't even come out yet, and might not be a success.'

'I doubt that.'

'You doubt what?'

'I think it is going to be a success. And I think this story was made for the silver screen.'

'You do?' said Joanne, unable to hide her surprise.

'Yes. When I was reading it, so many images came to my mind.'

'And . . . how do you picture it?'

'As a blockbuster adventure film. I worked for Warner Bros. in the USA. I'm sure they're going to love it.'

'I don't want an American film. *Harry Potter* is a British story. So if there ever was a film one day, as you say, it would be a British film. With British actors.'

'All right . . . of course, I understand,' David replied, shocked by the sudden turn the conversation had taken. Two seconds before, she had been on the verge of fainting, and then suddenly she had come out in firm defence of her work. When she spoke about *Harry Potter*, he felt the power of her conviction.

'Besides, you would need to make multiple films,' she went on. 'There are seven books. I've written them all already, in my head.'

13

In the middle of the night, Joanne awoke with a start, wondering if that bizarre conversation with the producer had really happened. She wasn't sure. But it had. They had spoken for more than an hour and promised to meet again soon. Which they did, over lunch, where the conversation continued as though it had never been interrupted. To prepare for the meeting, David had read the book a second time. It was always possible to talk money or casting to convince an author to sell the rights to their book, but the best way was to talk about the text. It showed his enthusiasm, which in turn made the author enthusiastic about him. David would soon receive a response from Warner Bros., who were willing to get involved. It was a huge coup, and proof that he was on the right track. All that remained was getting Joanne's agreement, but she was still overwhelmed by everything that was happening. Against all odds, the book was becoming a true phenomenon beyond her wildest dreams. The inevitable consequence of this would not be far behind: other significant production studios would begin to take an interest in the novel. David pressed Warner Bros. to act on his proposal; there was no time to lose. He spent several restless nights anguished at the thought of such a project passing him by. But Joanne reassured him at last: she wouldn't take any other meetings. He had been the first; he had been the one to believe in the story before it became a success, so it would be him. Yes, it would be him. They were now bound together by this adventure that would last a decade. David could hardly believe it; he had obtained the rights to a book that everyone in his profession dreamed of having. He felt as though he had bought the *Mona Lisa* while it was still a project in the mind of Leonardo da Vinci.

14

Everyone congratulated David on his outrageous achievement. The parents of the young producer were so proud of him.[3] However, objectively, nothing had yet been done. The world now expected a great film. First of all, they had to choose a director. Steven Spielberg was interested in the project, but only on the condition that he could make the film with Haley Joel Osment, the young actor famous for his role in *The Sixth Sense.*

---

3 Before long, they would regularly hear: 'Oh! You're David Heyman's parents!'

But Joanne wouldn't let go of the idea that the actors had to be British. In addition, she preferred Terry Gilliam, as did David. The former Monty Python star had made films before that were a little crazy, like *Brazil* and *The Adventures of Baron Munchausen*. They thought he could easily create the wizarding school's fantasy universe. But Warner Bros. quickly ruled him out: with his fiery reputation and excessive ego, things had the potential to explode. Later he would even be accused of being a cursed director, after numerous catastrophes on the set of *The Man Who Killed Don Quixote*. Though it was hard to imagine a more different candidate, next the studio thought of Chris Columbus, who'd just had back-to-back triumphs with *Home Alone* and *Mrs Doubtfire*. J. K. Rowling gave a faint smile, thinking that name had come straight from the *Harry Potter* universe, and admitted that it was a possibility. With experience of making family-friendly films, he was the sensible, unanimous choice. Most importantly, the producers wanted to secure their budget, which threatened to surpass a hundred million dollars. Thanks to the success of the book, everyone believed in the project now. There was an unusual buzz surrounding the preparation of the film.

For the role of Harry, David thought initially of Jamie Bell, who was soon to make his debut in *Billy Elliot*. David had seen the film at a private screening and was astounded at the young boy's performance. But he was thirteen, nearly fourteen – far too old, especially bearing in mind the series to come. Barring a complete disaster, filming would go on for years: it was essential to choose a ten-year-old for the first film. The quest for the perfect candidate promised to be difficult. The casting directors, Janet Hirshenson and Susie Figgis, got to work, auditioning dozens of young actors. As they knew the search would take time, it began, unusually, at the same time as the search for the screenwriter. Ordinarily, it is not until the screenplay is written that the hunt for the actors begins. Joanne didn't want to take on the task of writing the script. Not only did she think herself incapable of it, but she also wanted to concentrate on the next book. After much consideration, David thought of Richard Curtis, famous for the *Four Weddings and a Funeral* screenplay. A surprising choice, perhaps, but to David it wasn't incongruous to view *Harry Potter* as a comedy, or even a romantic comedy. He contacted Curtis, who invited him to drop in on the set of the film he had just written, *Notting Hill*. Screenwriters are rarely present on film sets, but this one was different; there were many personal elements in this particular script, down to the house it was filmed in, inspired by Richard's own. So he wanted to be on hand in case anybody needed him. In fact, he regretted not directing it himself. But he would direct his own stories soon enough: notably, in *Love Actually*.

15

And so David went to 104 Portobello Road, the house that served as the main backdrop. On set he greeted Hugh Grant, whom he knew well, but he couldn't spot Julia Roberts, though he would have loved to meet her; she didn't leave her dressing room in between takes. During the lunch break, David and Richard headed for a small Indian restaurant, which would be quieter than the canteen. In preparation, the producer had sent J. K. Rowling's novel to the screenwriter. They spoke of this and that (in other words, Julia Roberts), then Richard Curtis finally broached the main subject.

'I was rather surprised that you sent me this book. It's not really the sort of story people usually suggest to me.'

'I know.'

'That said, I was happy to read it. It's all anyone can talk about. And I can see why; it's very nicely done.'

'You know, I thought of you for the exact reasons that you find it incongruous. I'm sure that you would bring a truthfulness to Harry. To me, he is a child who is filled with wonder at what he discovers. It's not so far from what you write, the magic of emotions.'

'That's very kind. But honestly, there's too much wizardry in it for me.'

'Actually, I think the screenplay needs to be rooted in realism. The fantastical universe is already there – we need to accentuate the real. Children everywhere should recognise themselves in Harry Potter. At the beginning, when he is mistreated – that's a frustration that you know how to describe.'

'Yes, and his companion is a barn owl who's more intelligent than I am. This really isn't my area.'

'If you mean Hedwig, she's a snowy owl.'

'You see? I get mixed up between barn owls and snowy owls – that should tell you everything,' Richard said, grinning.

They continued the conversation lightheartedly for a while. Evidently, Curtis was not the right screenwriter. Frankly, he found the story far too long. There were too many elements, too many secondary characters, too many details you had to know in order to understand the Hogwarts universe. It would have to be an eight-hour-long film, in his opinion. In short, beyond his lack of interest, he didn't feel capable of such a task, and politely declined. In any case, he had an excellent excuse, which meant he wouldn't offend David or jeopardise any potential future collaborations.

'I've just been hired for a film that's going to take up a lot of my time. It's an adaptation too.'

'Which film?'

'*Bridget Jones's Diary.*'

Well, he could have told me that before agreeing to a meeting, thought David. It verged on rudeness. But Richard felt it was only polite to listen to David's proposal. There were, then, two ways of considering the same situation: the polite version, and the impolite one.

Looking back, David felt this exchange hadn't been completely useless; it had allowed him to refine his vision of the film. Curtis was right: the core of the project was fantasy. Seeing no other British screenwriters he could turn to, he began to think of American ones, notably, Steve Kloves. Without knowing anything about him, Joanne didn't seem keen on this idea. Once again: her story was a British one. To appease David, she nonetheless agreed to meet him. To everyone's great surprise, she was quickly convinced, and the contract was signed immediately. That evening, as they drank a glass of champagne in celebration, David went up to Joanne and asked her why she had changed her mind so easily. She looked at the producer, who was indisputably becoming a friend, and admitted: 'He told me his favourite character was Hermione.'

David paid the bill and escorted Richard back to set. He hadn't produced a film since he'd returned to London, and wanted to stay a while to watch the next scene. He missed the excitement; he couldn't stand any more days at the office or meetings in restaurants. As a child he had spent hours on set, trailing after his parents – that was what he loved. Whenever he was on a film set, he felt this childish wonder all over again – a time of innocence. And it was precisely in the midst of this bubble of nostalgia that he noticed, on the other side of the street, a small boy sitting on a chair. Round glasses, scruffy black hair. Frankly, it was like an apparition.

16

When thinking of the stroke of fate that placed Martin in David Heyman's path, with his glasses on his nose, no less, believing in witchcraft isn't much of a leap. But it was true. Every detail. It wasn't Martin who recounted this, but Susie Figgis, the casting director, in a behind-the-scenes documentary of the film broadcast by the BBC in 2011.

For now, the producer approached the young boy feverishly, almost unsteady on his feet. Standing in front of him, he searched for what to say, before deciding simply to introduce himself.

'Hello. My name is David. What's yours?'

'Martin.'

'And what are you doing here?'

'I'm going to be an extra in a bit.'

'Aren't all the extras in the same place? They're normally well away from the set.'

'I don't know. I'm here with my dad.'

'And who is your dad?'

'John Hill.'

'Is he working on the film?'

'Yes, he's a prop man.'

'Ah . . . I see. And do you like being an extra?'

'I don't really know. It hasn't started yet. My dad just told me I have to walk down the street in a little while.'

'Well, it's fun. You'll see. When I was young I loved coming on set with my parents too. Do you often come with your dad like this?'

'Hardly ever. It's just that Rose couldn't look after me.'

'And Rose is . . .?'

'My babysitter.'

David tried to stay calm, but he felt exhilarated. As well as his incredible physical resemblance to the character, the boy seemed to have a cool head. Other children, when questioned by an unknown adult in a strange environment, might have felt ill at ease. But not Martin. They talked some more about this and that. The producer didn't want to be too forward, but in the end he asked:

'Would you like to be an actor?'

'I don't know.'

'Acting in a film. Playing a character, not just an extra. Do you think that would be fun?'

'. . .'

At that moment, John came over and interrupted the conversation.

'Hello, I'm Martin's father. Is there a problem?'

'No, no, not at all. My name is David Heyman. I'm a producer. I was just having a chat with Martin.'

'Yes, I can see that,' John said sharply, clearly finding it suspicious that this man was accosting his son like this.

'I'd love to talk to you, if possible,' added David.

'Talk to me about what?'

'I was just asking Martin if he would be interested in acting.'

'My son?'

'Yes.'

Someone called to John, for something that seemed to require an urgent response.

'I have to go. We're filming soon.'

'Yes, of course, I understand. I'll give you my card, and we can talk when you have a quiet moment tonight, if you like. Or whenever you can.'

John took David's card, told Martin that they would soon be

filming the scene where he had to walk down the street, and ran off again. Martin had never seen him so stressed. Normally his father was nonchalance personified, but he was clearly under a lot of pressure on this shoot. David spoke to Martin a while longer, but without mentioning *Harry Potter*. He wanted to have that conversation in a calmer, less pressurised setting. In the end, David didn't have time to wait for the next scene; he had to return to the office. He shook Martin's hand and said, emphatically, 'See you soon.' As unbelievable as it might seem, as he left the set, he came face to face with Julia Roberts. It was a sign that something miraculous had just occurred.

17

John waited until his son was in bed before phoning David Heyman. David was outside in the street when he picked up; the sounds of the city confirmed it. At the time, mobile phones were still a gadget for the rich, a device reserved for those who wanted to emphasise their own importance. John thought furtively that he would have loved to have invented it himself, before concentrating on what the producer was saying. David certainly wasn't a pervert, as John had thought initially. In truth, John's intuition had always been pitiful. When asked who would win the next election, he would give the name of the loser without fail. Earlier that day he had rushed up to this man, cutting him off mid-conversation, instantly imagining he was horribly depraved. When, in fact, the producer just wanted his son to do a screen test – for *Harry Potter*. That was his proposal. He had seen in John's son a potential actor for the film he was going to make; and moreover, in his opinion, Martin's resemblance to the main character was staggering.

Who Harry Potter was, on the other hand, John hadn't the slightest idea. Since Jeanne had left, he no longer followed the news. The phenomenon had completely passed him by. It was his wife who used to keep the family in touch with reality. Now, there was no reason to pay attention to current affairs. Sometimes John even felt as though his mind was stuck in 1992 or 1993, wedged somewhere between his two happy days.

After he hung up, he went into Martin's room and watched him sleep. When Martin was a baby, John often went to check his breathing, and as the years went on, he had never given up this night-time ritual. Nothing could compare to the sight of his son being soothed by his dreams. Such contemplation could drive away all resentment. At that moment, reality presented itself in all its dazzling simplicity, stripped of uncertainty. John was fascinated by how deeply children slept. You could play the clarinet in their ear (which would be unlikely, admittedly, except in families of music-loving maniacs), and they would remain immersed in their impenetrable nocturnal world. Perhaps that was the greatest strength of childhood, the ability to sleep soundly. Nothing can happen to us when we sleep like this. At what point in life do we lose this ability – around fourteen or fifteen years old? Perhaps the crisis of adolescence stems from this, this loss of uninterrupted rest. John hadn't slept like that for such a long time. Never again would he know the depths of the night, where nothing from the day is retained.

That night was no exception. John lay awake, replaying the producer's words in his mind. David had seemed so sure of his instincts. This was how future stars were often discovered – by accident. A short time ago, he had heard such a story about Bruce Willis: his career took off after he caught a casting director's eye while working as a barman in Los Angeles. In the maze of his nocturnal thoughts, John was already imagining himself in the front row of a film preview. But he knew the score. How many broken promises and dashed hopes had there been in the history of cinema? Yet, it was possible to be realistic while letting himself indulge in a fantasy. There was no reason not to embrace one certainty in a world of hypotheticals. So he continued to imagine the best-case scenario. Which, logically, involved Jeanne's return to London. Surely she would come back to be close to her son, and their relationship would have a second chance. It was with this image in mind that John fell asleep, as if dreaming his way into his dreams.

18

The next morning, John made his son's breakfast, but felt it wasn't the right moment to speak to him. To his mind, what he had to say was not a 'sitting-down conversation'. It was only on the way to school that he told Martin about his conversation with the producer.

'Of course I know *Harry Potter*! Everyone at school is reading it,' Martin replied immediately. Two short sentences that emphasised to John how out of touch he was. Every day he became more aware of how he had avoided current trends. So he explained the situation to his son. The man who had come to speak to him on set thought he looked a lot like the main character, news which Martin found incredible. If he hadn't felt curious about it up until that moment, now he was dying to get stuck into the book. Did he really look like Harry? No one had ever said anything like that to him before.

Once they arrived outside the school, John got to the heart of the matter.

'Do you think it would be fun to do a screen test?'

'What's that?'

'You act in front of a camera, and they see if you're a good fit.'

'But I'm not an actor.'

'Sometimes, they hire people who aren't professionals for films. If they explain it to you, I'm sure you'll be able to do it.'

'I don't know.'

'If you ask me, there's no harm in trying. And it could definitely be fun.'

Much later, Martin would think back to that conversation, particularly those words of his father's: 'it could definitely be fun'. They sent a shiver down his spine. Hardly surprising, given the havoc the audition was going to wreak.

Just like his father the night before, Martin spent the school day fantasising about the best-case scenario. In between arithmetic exercises, he saw himself as a film star, maybe even making an appearance in Michael Jackson's next music video. Everyone would look at him starry-eyed, and Betty would be kicking herself for having turned him down. Magnanimously, he would forgive her initial mistake, and they would fall in love after all. In fact, Martin was looking far off into the future, in terms of the possible consequences of his success. John, his feet firmly on the ground, told his son that nothing was confirmed yet. It was just an audition, nothing more. And moreover, he added, there would probably be dozens of children fighting for the role. But that didn't stop Martin from dreaming, the way a lottery player starts thinking about what they will buy with their future fortune as they choose their numbers.

19

That evening, father and son decided to skim the first few chapters of the book together. John had gone to buy it in his lunch break; immediately inside the door of the bookshop, a stack of J. K. Rowling books awaited each new customer. Success breeds success, and you could no longer reach any other book without passing by the *Harry Potter* section. Though he was a Russian literature enthusiast who had never ventured into the children's or fantasy departments, John was nonetheless drawn in by the story. He particularly enjoyed the author's sense of humour, smiling at every mention of the ridiculous Dursleys. John even recognised himself in the young Harry, his life marred by injustice. In truth, everyone felt this same connection with the novel's hero. There was something universal in the pages of the book. Harry Potter represented our rebellious side, our desire to have powers to defeat the bad guys, our dreams of a better life.

For Martin, the connection was even more obvious. Every word was proof that this book was about him. Now he understood what the producer had felt. It was true – the descriptions of Harry, of his hair, his general mannerisms, really resonated with him. Doubtless, all Martin needed to do was to pick up a magic wand to become the young wizard. But the resemblance didn't stop him from preparing for the meeting. The screen test was scheduled for the following Monday, which didn't give him much time, particularly as he would be in Paris at the weekend. That only left them two evenings to try and anticipate what they would ask him to do. John pushed all the furniture in the living room to the side to give them space to move, ordered a huge pizza, and assumed the role of drama teacher.

'At the beginning of the novel, two main emotions are apparent: the first, of course, is sadness. And I'm being kind – you could really call it suffering. Poor Harry, who is already an orphan, is mistreated by his aunt and uncle, and their awful son, Dulley.'

'Dudley,' Martin corrected him.

'Ah yes, Dudley. Sorry. Anyway, it will be that emotion they'll want to see from you. Harry is trapped in a world where he can't do anything. The second emotion, I think, is wonder. You are about to discover an extraordinary, unimaginable world. There's the scene with the snake at the zoo, but it mainly starts with the arrival of Hagrid the giant—'

'He's a half-giant, Dad.'

'Right, right. This is good, kiddo, you've remembered all the details . . . Now, where was I?'

'Wonder.'

'Yes, that was it. On your birthday, you find out you're a world-famous wizard. Can you imagine? It's crazy. So, those are the two emotions we are going to explore this evening: sadness and wonder. Which one do you want to start with?'

'Sadness, maybe?'

'Great. So, tell me what makes you sad.'

'Well . . . thinking about you and Maman breaking up.'

'Actually, maybe we'd better start with wonder.'

After that sticky moment, Martin let himself be guided by his father's instructions:

'Imagine you're at the station, looking for Platform 9 ¾. There you go, that's it . . . You're thinking it's all a load of rubbish . . . and then, suddenly, you get it! You see other children walking through the wall, and you try it too. That's it . . . imagine you're charging at a wall you could crash into, but no! Hey presto! You've passed through it! Come on, let's go, kiddo . . .' Martin stifled a laugh at his father's excitement as he shook his arms in every direction, but he went along with the game and mimed moving through an invisible wall. 'Oh yes, that's it! Bravo!' John enthused. They looked like two madmen, trying to act out a blockbuster film in a twenty-square-metre living room. But it was so much fun. They were enjoying themselves more than they had in a long time, almost forgetting why they were doing it in the first place. John was discovering a new side to his son; he was inventive, and had a particular sense of humour. It was hard to say if he was witnessing the birth of a true gift, but something was certainly happening. Sometimes, when playing a role, we end up finding ourselves. Formerly a child with no real passion for anything, Martin now dreamed of signing up to a drama class. Of course, the enthusiasm he had seen on the producer's face was a deciding factor. We always prefer to go where we are wanted. Whether he had chosen it or not, the exercise had at least revealed this to Martin: he wanted to be an actor.

20

On Friday evening, the pair said their goodbyes at Waterloo Station where, until 2007, the Eurostar departed from. Martin, who had become accustomed to travelling alone, viewed these journeys as a taster of adult life. He felt conflicted. Martin thought about his father as he unfolded the tinfoil to eat the sandwich he had prepared for him. It broke his heart to leave him alone; he always felt a little guilty about going to meet his mother. But that didn't stop him from being glad for her. He knew she was much happier since she had returned to live in France; her smile had come back. Martin went back and forth like this between his parents' emotions, between bitterness and hope, still not knowing where to land. An emotional turmoil exacerbated by the knowledge that he was on a train speeding below the sea.

When she picked him up that Friday, Jeanne held her son tightly in her arms – perhaps a little too tightly, as though her body had to make up for the days they hadn't seen each other. After this embrace, she stepped back.

'It's so strange seeing you with glasses, darling!' She added that it gave him the air of John Lennon. No doubt about it – he looked much more like an English boy than a French boy. In the battle of genes, his father had won.

Martin wanted to ask her, 'Don't you think I look like Harry Potter?' but he decided to wait a bit longer before talking to her about it. He had already kept the news from her for several days, not wanting to recount this extraordinary adventure over the phone and miss seeing the look on his mother's face. The apartment was a ten-minute walk away. Jeanne had rented a flat in a 1970s building that was rather charmless, but had the advantage of being close to the station, which was logistically useful and reduced the time spent travelling. In order to further limit the trauma of all this change, she had done her best to decorate Martin's room in Paris exactly like his room in England. Everything was the same, from the wallpaper to the duvet cover. Martin understood that she had done this with the best of intentions, and so did not want to upset her by telling her that he found it frankly bizarre. It gave him the feeling of having travelled a long way only to end up in exactly the same place.

Once he had put his bag down, Martin declared enigmatically, 'There's something I need to tell you.' His mother was immediately worried – it had to be bad news. In reassuring her, he dragged out the pleasure of the announcement. Once she had heard the whole story, Jeanne was both stunned and not surprised at all. Of course her son was marvellous, and blessed with a rare charisma.

In the end she said, decisively, 'I'm sure they'll choose you!' Martin had to temper her enthusiasm, explaining that the casting in question was the biggest one in Britain right now. 'Oh really? The biggest casting . . . So what's this film called?'

'*Harry Potter.*'

'Harry who?'

'Potter.'

'Never heard of it.'

The phenomenon hadn't yet crossed the Channel. On Monday, Jeanne made enquiries in the cultural section of her newspaper and discovered that the French translation was to be published imminently on Gallimard's Folio Junior list. Impressed by the incredible success of the novel in Britain, she offered to write an article about this woman who had gone from unemployment to stardom in a matter of weeks. As such, Martin Hill's mother became the first journalist to write about J. K. Rowling in France.

Above and beyond the promise of a wonderful adventure, Jeanne was even happier to see her son's enthusiasm. She often worried about him, tortured by the thought of having abandoned him in London. So she too drifted into daydreaming. She was ready to ignore reality entirely if she could see her son happy. You might even say that a kind of magic had taken hold of their lives, as something happened the next day that was almost fateful. As they were walking along the Seine, they found themselves in front of the Shakespeare and Company bookshop, where an English copy of Harry Potter sat in the middle of the window. They went inside the shop to buy the book. As they were paying, the bookseller sighed:

'I remember her very well.'

'Who? The author?' Jeanne asked.

'Yes. When I saw her photo on the marketing insert that came with the delivery, I recognised her right away. She was a student at the Sorbonne and used to hang around the bookshop nearly every day.'

'That's amazing!' said Martin. 'What was she like?'

'Quite mysterious. She could spend an hour just looking at book covers, as though she was more fascinated by the objects themselves than their contents. I tried to speak to her a few times, but she was very shy.'

'. . .'

'Are you going to buy that?' he asked after a moment, snapping immediately back to the pragmatic.

In light of what he had just learned, Martin looked around the place as though it had suddenly become magical. J. K. Rowling had come here, and she must still exist in the memory of the walls. The evening before, as the Eurostar carried him to Paris, he had finished the book in a kind of ecstasy. He had never read a book so quickly. Of course, the audition had given him an extra reason to devour the story, but it was more than that. He had felt such a connection with the characters, as though it was possible to become friends with fictional creations. Martin had joined the ever-growing bunch of groupies. So yes, it was a thrill for him to find these traces of J. K. Rowling, to walk in her footsteps. He dreamed now of meeting her.

21

Jeanne didn't see the point of having her son for the weekend if she was going to leave him in the care of a babysitter, so she took him with her everywhere. That Saturday evening, she was going to dinner at her friends' house. 'It'll be fun, you'll see,' she had hastily promised. 'There will be lots of other children there.' A totally false statement, as there was only one six-year-old boy present. Upon his arrival, Martin understood that he would have to look after this kid, particularly as said kid was fascinated by the presence of someone older. The two of them had dinner together, away from the adults, in a bedroom while watching cartoons. Jeanne checked on her son regularly, asking if everything was okay. He said yes, to be polite, and so as not to ruin her evening. Her face was made up, and she was wearing a beautiful dress – her new era seemed to be manifesting itself physically. When she came out of the bathroom all dolled up Martin had barely recognised her, and almost asked if they were going to a fancy-dress party.

When they arrived, Martin said hello to everyone, in that polite manner that makes children look like monkeys trained to shine in company. There were two couples, and a single man in his forties. The man had been particularly attentive to him. Or he had tried, at least. He seemed ill at ease with any human specimen under twenty years old. He was one of those adults who speak to children as though they are half-wits, enunciating every syllable: 'Hel-lo Mar-tin! My name is Marc and I am ve-ry pleased to meet you!' – as if he was speaking in Morse code. Jeanne stood at her son's side, seeming uncomfortable. Out of nowhere, rather awkwardly, Marc suddenly announced that he too loved Arsenal football club. But after two sentences on the subject, it was obvious that he didn't know much about football — he had simply wanted to try and buy Martin's allegiance by mentioning some pseudo-common ground.

Soon enough, Martin would be able to decipher this odd exchange. It was the behaviour of a man trying to please a child to win over a woman. Deep down, this made him rather likeable. Marc would have acted the same way if Jeanne had had a dog, and would have patted its back, exclaiming, 'Good boy, good boy!' When they left, he shook Martin's hand, as though role-playing a relationship of one man to another, and kissed Jeanne on the cheek while touching her back. A rather emphatic touch, as though refusing to accept the code discouraging public displays of affection.

In the taxi back to the apartment, Jeanne asked:

'So, did you like Marc?'

'Yeah, he was okay.'

'Well, he thought you were adorable. And he has a huge house in the country. Maybe we could go there when the weather is nice?'

'Sure, if you want.'

Once in bed, Martin thought again about that man's hand on his mother's back. She was free to start a new relationship, of course – he knew that. But when he thought of his father, the idea tortured him. Martin knew John secretly hoped things would still work out, that the separation would be temporary; he was lying to himself, in the same way he had always invented ideas about his life. Therein surely lay his true talent for invention. Martin was probably similar, good at imagining something better, good at dreaming about his life instead of living it. No wonder he felt so connected to Harry Potter; he had inherited a sort of incompatibility with reality, an ease with the world of the imaginary. But the facts had still caught up with him, and Martin began to cry silently for his father. He kept seeing the image of that man touching his mother's back. A throwaway gesture, but through it he had understood that the past was definitively behind him.

22

The following Monday, John went to meet his son at the school gates. They had a meeting at five o'clock with the casting director. Before we get to this meeting, however, one last rather strange coincidence must be mentioned. Two weeks earlier, the new headteacher, evidently a conservative man, had decided that from then on all students must wear a uniform, even though, in this state school, the students had always demanded the right to choose how they dressed, rejecting one of those British traditions that still prevailed elsewhere. Faced with an outcry, he had given way somewhat, insisting simply that the students wear a jacket. So, each morning Martin now put on a navy-blue blazer with its crest in the school colours. Kitted out like this, along with his hair and glasses, he looked as if he had walked straight out of Hogwarts. Every day, it seemed that chance was pushing him closer to the role. In fact, when he arrived at the production offices, Susie Figgis welcomed him with the words: 'Ah! What a great idea, wearing a blazer!' It's always disconcerting when you get it exactly right despite yourself.

Susie was a warm, jolly woman – it was clear that she truly loved her job. She must have gone to every amateur dramatics production in every suburb of London, in the hope of unearthing a gem who would become the next Kenneth Branagh or Alan Parker. The constant lure of discovery was at the heart of her job: the urge to be the one who recognised the genius of an unknown actor before anyone else. In the casting process for *Harry Potter*, she got more than she had bargained for. It was by far the most exciting assignment she had ever been given. The flipside was the enormous pressure she was under from Warner Bros. Everyone felt that the film, grand as it might be with its impressive sets and mind-blowing special effects, would be a hollow shell without the right Harry. She was tasked with finding the linchpin of the whole endeavour. What's more, the process was well underway for the other roles. At this stage, Hermione had almost been cast, and Ron would soon follow suit. It was just Harry, still Harry, who was missing. Susie and Janet, the other casting director, had already auditioned so many hopefuls, but there was always something not quite right. Either the actor wasn't up to the job, or he didn't look enough like the character. Or he was too old, or too young. Some candidates were still in the running, but there were no serious leads. And they weren't about to spend hundreds of millions of dollars on a 'maybe'.

On the way to the audition, John had warned his son, 'You know, people in power tend to abuse it. Don't let that unsettle you. What counts is what's within you.' It's difficult to imagine a pep talk less rooted in reality. Susie had immediately shown great kindness, and had tried to put Martin at ease. Just like David Heyman, she could clearly see there was something special about this new hopeful. She hardly dared believe it, but perhaps it was Harry who had just crossed the threshold of her office. Before starting, she asked her assistant, Edward, to come and film the audition. When he entered the room, she didn't even turn around. She couldn't take her eyes off Martin. She prayed that he would pass the screen test. But she also knew that with a good coach, and a lot of takes on set, you could turn anyone into an actor. Of course, it would be easier to achieve the desired result with someone who had talent, but anything was possible. Physical resemblance was already a large part of the job. Which was why the first thing Susie mentioned was:

'You really have the look we've been searching for.'

'. . .'

'Have you ever acted before?'

'No, never.'

'Well, we practised a bit last week,' John interjected, earning himself a cold look from Susie; she was used to intrusive parents at under-age castings.

'What did you do?'

'Some exercises—'

'I'm asking Martin,' the casting director cut him off, rather irritated at this second interruption.

John apologised. He felt foolish at having responded for his son once again, and risking ruining the moment. How could they imagine Martin as the hero of such a film if his father spoke for him? But he was anxious on his behalf. Since the previous Wednesday, he had been downplaying it, claiming that it would be 'fun just doing the audition', but all this was making him more nervous than he would care to admit. But there was no need to be. Everything was going well. Once his father fell quiet, Martin managed perfectly. Susie asked him some questions about his life and his hobbies, then moved on to more serious things. John was pleased to see that what the casting director asked Martin to act out was exactly what they had practised: one of the scenes where Harry is mistreated.

'In the book, Harry is really the family's punchbag. Even worse, his awful cousin's favourite pastime is "Harry-hunting" with his friends. Have you read the book?' asked Susie.

'Yes.'

'Very good. In any case, don't worry – we aren't going to go "Martin-hunting"! Edward is just going to say some . . . rather nasty things to you, and you just react as you see fit. Either by speaking or through facial expressions. Does that sound okay?'

'Yes, okay.'

The assistant took out a sheet and stood up to deliver the insults. Martin suppressed a fit of the giggles – this hadn't started well – but then he managed to control himself. To be like Harry, he mustn't react aggressively. In the book, it was clear that the hero had an even-tempered way of letting the hatred wash over him. That was his strength; they had no hold over him. So Martin dodged the attacks, responding evasively, even with humour. Susie seemed pleasantly surprised. She intervened on occasion to clarify an instruction, or to give him something to do. Martin began to forget why he was there, and took evident pleasure in being directed in this way. The casting director then asked him to improvise a sort of rebellious tirade. 'Even if it has nothing to do with the story, tell me what annoys you! Tell me what gets on your nerves!' This was more difficult; nothing really angered him. Surely he couldn't talk about Arsenal's recent defeat? Eventually, it was by thinking of football that he began to talk about Quidditch, the sport played by the young witches and wizards. He got angry just by changing the language – raging against the referee hidden behind a cloud, or the use of a defective broomstick. At the end of his rant, which had certainly been risky, everyone congratulated him. He had shown a real inventiveness, a major quality and asset for an actor.

John noted with satisfaction that Edward and Susie kept throwing each other knowing looks. He wished he could have shared this moment with Jeanne. But he had to stay focused, because Susie went on:

'Now I'm going to ask you something difficult, and it's not a big deal if you can't do it.'

'Okay.'

'You're going to try to cry. Generally, actors think about sad things in their own lives, but it's not a foolproof technique. Sometimes it's simply mechanical, as if turning on the taps inside your eyes.'

Martin smiled at the thought of this image, which was not the ideal way to achieve the concentration he needed to make the tears come. He glanced at his father, looking for encouragement. Then he became thoughtful. What memory could he think about? It was such a strange situation. Three people were staring at him, waiting for him to cry. And that's exactly what he did. After about a minute, the liquid miracle began to flow.

Susie approached him and gave him a friendly pat on the back. She tried to hide the excitement that had taken hold of her. It was important not to give false hope, especially to a young actor. Even though she herself was utterly thrilled, the decision wasn't hers to make. Chris Columbus and J. K. Rowling might have a different perspective on what had happened when they watched the screen test. But she didn't think so. This boy was incredible; it would surely be unanimous. She worked with him a little more, on some lighter things. Martin acted out the wonderment of his arrival at Hogwarts. He improvised again with elements taken from the book, adding references here and there, and even began a sort of conversation with Hedwig, Harry Potter's owl. It was remarkably sophisticated; his eagerness and his ability were indisputable.

It was almost seven o'clock when the session came to a close. They said goodbye on the landing with big smiles and promises that they would 'be in touch very soon'. Once outside, John congratulated his son.

'You cried, can you believe it? You cried! It's amazing!'

'Yeah, I'm pleased about that!'

'And two hours, can you believe it? That went on for two hours. It's a very good sign. Do you think that woman would have wasted two hours of her time for nothing?'

'. . .'

'Two hours, can you believe it?'

Martin was happy to see his father's enthusiasm, but more importantly he felt in himself that it had gone well. He was relieved. Too excited to go home, they went to get cheeseburgers at their favourite fast-food restaurant, rehashing the audition in detail throughout the meal. Once home, John dashed to the phone: 'Come on, we have to tell Maman all about it!' It would finally be an opportunity to talk about something positive. But nobody picked up. They tried again half an hour later, but the phone rang out once more into thin air. John hid his distress, but the knowledge that Jeanne was out at this time of night obviously somewhat marred the happiness he felt. He imagined her at a restaurant, having dinner with a man. In actual fact, she was dying to hear the news, but she had been kept late at the offices of the newspaper by an interminable editorial board meeting. First thing the next morning, she would phone her son so he could tell her everything.

23

As for Susie, she had called David the second Martin and his father had left her office. He came to watch the audition immediately; while in front of the screen, he hadn't given anything away. At the end, he turned slowly towards his casting director, and looked her straight in the eye – a look that said, 'That's it! We've just found our bloody Harry!'

24

For once, Martin had trouble falling asleep. Although he had set out on this adventure casually, now he could no longer contain his excitement. He couldn't stop thinking about the incredible life he was about to embark on. It was madness, what was happening. He tried to reason with himself, to remind himself that nothing was definite yet – but in vain. His mind explored all the possibilities, progressively destroying the barrier between dream and reality. He had glimpsed the life of a film star on the set of *Notting Hill*. He had seen the aura that surrounded the actors; the excitement when they passed, the way people held their breath. Who wouldn't fantasise about being adored like that? That was what they were offering him. One thing led to another, and he was soon imagining himself in the VIP box at Arsenal matches. He might even be friends with the players. He would travel the world – by private jet, no doubt – and could buy an enormous apartment where he would throw big parties. He drifted for a long time in this ultimate version of his future. He was dying to tell his friends, to shout from the rooftops about what was happening. But his father had advised him to keep quiet for the moment. Thinking too much about it could end up putting the whole thing under too much pressure and interfere with the outcome. It was better to be discreet and only announce the good news in a great blaze of glory once everything was signed. All the same, keeping a cool head was becoming very difficult. The adventure seemed so real now; a miraculous life awaited him.

25

Fate is decidedly cruel. Before crossing paths with Martin, David Heyman had his heart set on another actor. He had noticed a certain Daniel Radcliffe in a BBC TV film about David Copperfield. He had also already met Daniel's father, who was a literary agent. Despite this connection, things weren't that simple. There was talk of making seven films, probably in Los Angeles. After some reflection, the parents of young Daniel had therefore decided that their son would not attend the screen test for *Harry Potter*. It would be too great an upheaval; it would mean dropping out of school. The producer had insisted, but there was nothing to be done: the answer was no.

Even so, fate had decided otherwise, and chose to throw the two together once more. During a performance of the play *Stones in His Pockets*, David Heyman spotted Daniel and his parents a few seats away. It was surely a sign. However, the play told the story of a small town taken over by the shooting of a Hollywood film, culminating in the suicide of an extra who'd been rejected by the lead actress. In short, this drama about the destructive power of cinema was not the ideal setting. But David wasn't too worried. He spent the play with his head turned towards his prey.

They met at the exit. After a few polite exchanges, David mentioned *Harry Potter* again. He didn't beat around the bush.

'I have to insist . . . We would really love to have Daniel audition.'

'We know,' responded his mother. 'But we don't want Dan to be out of school for such a long time.'

His parents had agreed that Daniel could do a few films – and maybe he would want to become an actor later on – but for the moment, their priority was his education. But a simple meeting wouldn't commit him to anything, and could only be useful experience for his career progression, David argued. And the situation was different now: there was a good chance that the filming would take place in London. Daniel Radcliffe's father would later recount that everything had hinged on that chance second meeting. When he saw the producer again, he thought, 'Perhaps fate is trying to tell us something.' So they agreed that Daniel could audition.

They chatted for a while longer outside the theatre, David shooting glances at Daniel. In the end, he asked him:

'Have you read the book?'

'Yes.'

'Did you like it?'

'Of course.'

'What was your favourite part of the story?'

'I like that Harry's parents are dead. Being an orphan sounds pretty good to me,' he said, grinning at his mum and dad.

26

By all accounts, Daniel's audition was rather poor. Despite the impression he had given with his humorous remark outside the theatre, he was a reserved child. This wasn't, of course, necessarily a disadvantage when it came to playing Harry Potter, but his demeanour sometimes bordered on that of an introvert. Later on, Daniel himself would admit in numerous interviews how badly he thought the first meeting had gone. By the time he got home, he had almost forgotten about it already. It was over.

So he was surprised to get a callback. Of course, everyone

had been enthusiastic about Martin Hill, but it was always best to have multiple options. Daniel felt instinctively that opportunity was knocking. He wasn't wrong; if they wanted to see him again after his poor showing, it had to be a good sign. The whole team felt that he looked so much like the character it would be absurd not to give him another chance. This time, his desire to be chosen was clearly much stronger. He prepared for the audition with his mother. As she was a casting director herself, Daniel benefited from her vast experience. Unlike Martin's audition, footage of this second camera test is easy to find. Without knowing it, this shy, smiling child was on the brink of stardom. Dressed in the outfit of a sorcerer's apprentice, with his round glasses and a wand in his hand, there was no doubt about it: Daniel Radcliffe had become a very serious contender for the role.

The most complex part of the affair then began. Daniel's parents learned that there were only two young actors still in the running. Their son was in competition with a certain Martin Hill. As they had never heard of him before, they made some enquiries. He was the son of a prop designer who had been found by chance on a film set, and wasn't an actor at all. An atypical profile – he must have real talent to have made it this far. Although initially reluctant, Radcliffe's parents were starting to get swept up in the excitement after the second audition. They had now come to the conclusion that this role would be an incredible opportunity for their son. Daniel himself had already started dreaming of what could be. All his friends had read the book, and he imagined their faces when he told them he was going to be Harry Potter. It would be simply amazing.

The two finalists were summoned for another audition, this time with a script to learn, in front of Chris Columbus. The director, who had worked with Macaulay Culkin, knew how to direct children and get the best out of them. He had been captivated by both performances, had weighed the pros and cons, and concluded that the decision would be very difficult. It would be best to move on to the next stage: an audition with the other actors. Seeing the chemistry between the trio would help them choose. Emma Watson had got the role of Hermione. The process had been very easy – she had immediately stood out from the other girls. During her audition, she had shown herself to be both mischievous and focused. On top of that, it was clear that she was dying to be chosen. Her energy had blown them all away. During the first press conference, where the actors were introduced to the world, even before filming had started, there was no doubt about it: Emma Watson had the makings of a star. For Ron, the road had been a little longer. Rupert Grint had initially auditioned for the role of Harry, before being cast in that of his affectionate, steadfast friend.

So Daniel Radcliffe and then Martin Hill found themselves face to face with Rupert Grint and Emma Watson. Their task was a tricky one: they had to immediately convince everyone that these two strangers were their best friends. Daniel did the best at this game. Having already acted in a film, he had the necessary experience to interact with his co-stars. He laughed at Ron's jokes and let himself be guided by Hermione's energy. The trio worked; it was indisputable. But for the rest of the audition, he was a little too withdrawn, as if he were afraid of stealing the limelight from the others. Actually, that was just his way of being, and in the end it was quite in keeping with the attitude of Harry Potter, apprehensive at having discovered an unknown world.

Next, it was Martin's turn. Things didn't go quite as well for him. He felt suddenly crushed by the weight of expectation.

It was too important a moment to manage with ease. When the time came for him to act, his legs began to shake. Why hadn't he felt this way last time? Everything was different now that victory seemed to be within reach. It wasn't at all like the first audition, when he'd had nothing to lose – now he had everything to lose. His vision, too, began to blur. He felt everyone's eyes on him, waiting for him to start speaking. The two other actors tried to encourage him. Even though they could relax now that they had been selected, the memory of their recent stage fright was still fresh in their minds. Eventually the director approached Martin to comfort him: it's no big deal, it happens to all actors, even the most experienced ones. Do you want to take a break? Have a drink of something? Martin tried to smile, but his jaw was no longer working. He felt so ashamed; he had already pictured himself as Harry. More than that: he felt he was Harry. The night before he had read the book again, feeling closer than ever to the character. And there was another element to it: before the audition, they had shown him some models of the sets. Hogwarts and its Great Hall had materialised before him. This had certainly added to his anxiety; he had looked his dream straight in the eye.

It is so easy to give up. We stop trying, cutting short the ordeal with our dignity more or less intact. But that wasn't the case for Martin. His emotions did a U-turn, and he found a second wind. The session was restarted, and things went much better. Martin could have kicked himself for having given such a bad impression, but his capacity to overcome his fear was commendable. What's more, Columbus seemed surprised by this turnaround, which perhaps worked in Martin's favour. It is particularly impressive to succeed at something after having initially failed at it. The three children had to act out a scene in which Hermione reveals her discoveries about a man called Nicolas Flamel. Ron and Harry had to ask her questions, and comment on her answers. For a few minutes, they all left reality behind them, swept up as they were in J. K. Rowling's world. Everything seemed trivial and fun, though what they were doing could change their lives. A child's game with adult consequences.

27

At the end of the session, Martin felt great, as though galvanised by the fantastical world. He wanted to act again and again. He imagined other scenes, with adventure and twists and turns. In any case, he could be satisfied; after a slow start, he had managed to give the best of himself. Everyone had said kind things. But was that just to reassure him? No, it seemed sincere. Rupert had congratulated him, and Emma had added that it was 'super cool' acting with him. Chris Columbus had spent a long time chatting with him about the role. The future seemed so certain.

However, the scale was tipping in Daniel's favour. But it wasn't as simple as that. The production company's decision would be final, and would dictate the whole destiny of the planned series. They gauged the assets and flaws of both candidates, who were terribly well balanced. The representatives from Warner made the journey from the USA, and organised an important meeting in London with David Heyman, Chris Columbus, and of course, J. K. Rowling, who each gave their opinion. Much later, in an interview with the *Huffington Post* which can easily be found on the internet, one of the casting directors summarised what really happened at that time. Janet

Hirshenson said that while Martin looked the part and had Harry's vulnerability, they needed the actor to have two sides. Daniel Radcliffe also possessed a powerful quality that was necessary to play Harry Potter.

That was why Daniel Radcliffe had been chosen. It was a question of intuition: he would have the mental strength to endure such an extreme experience. But there was something else. In her statement, the casting director had used an interesting phrase: 'both sides'. Another ineffable quality that was nonetheless decisive. If Martin had asked, 'Why him, and not me?' they would have told him it was all down to that mysterious other side he lacked.

Losing something so great over something so small is enough to make anyone go mad.

This is how a human life can tip over to the wrong side. It is always something insignificant that makes the difference, the way the simple positioning of a comma can change the meaning of an eight-hundred-page novel.

28

Now they had to let the two finalists know. First the good news: reassuring the chosen winner. Then they had to turn their attention to the loser. No doubt Martin Hill's disappointment would be immense. No one could have imagined just how painful it would be.

Right now, Daniel is lounging in a bubble bath, playing with a rubber duck that has grown mouldy over the years. He should really have thrown it away, but it is hard to get rid of the relics of childhood. For days, he has been paralysed by waiting, and his parents feel the same. So he spends his time splashing around, as though the hours might pass more quickly in the water. Suddenly, he hears the telephone ringing. One ring, then two, then three – why isn't his father picking up? If this goes on he will have to get out of the bath and rush to the living room to answer the call, but no, no need, it's fine, he hears his father answer it at last. He is motionless, trying to hear – does it have anything to do with him, to do with the casting? He can't wait any longer, it's torture; why is his father speaking so quietly, he can't hear a thing – that can't be a good sign, it has to be a bad sign; when you hear good news you celebrate, even shouting with joy, particularly for this kind of news. But there is nothing, not a sound, no reaction, as if there's been a death in the living room, and the conversation goes on, and on, even though his father normally hates talking on the phone. The water is cold now, it's uncomfortable, the moment becomes unbearable, but Daniel suddenly imagines that if he gets out of the water he won't get the part, that it had just been a fancy passing through his head, a strange mind game, but that's the way it is, he has to stay in the bath until he knows what the phone call is about. This has to work. His father hangs up at last, but nothing happens, a silence takes hold, he's evidently gone back into his office; so it wasn't a call from the production company, still nothing, still nothing, still nothing, he is still stuck in limbo, he's no longer completely Daniel, nor yet Harry. All this waiting is a bad sign, it's stupid to keep believing, it's screwed, totally screwed, but in the midst of this wave of negativity he hears footsteps approaching, yes, there are footsteps coming towards him, his father must want to speak to him, yes, no doubt about it, in a moment he will open the door. Daniel stares at the door handle, his thoughts running riot, a confusion of all the possible outcomes, why is his father coming now; at least the chaos of uncertainty is short, he is finally opening the door with a look on his face Daniel has never seen before, as if a stranger is standing before him, motionless, it is a look full of gravity, and he lets the silence linger for a few moments before breaking it.

'You got it.'

29

Some years earlier, David Heyman had received a letter from Olga, his Russian girlfriend. She had been his first great love, the one you are condemned to remember for the rest of your life. They had met as teenagers and had enjoyed several wonderful months together. But in the end, she had decided to finish it – by letter. It's well known that Russians have a literary bent. David had not forgotten the terrible feeling of his heart hammering as he opened an envelope from his beloved, finding himself faced with words of rejection. He could say nothing back. A letter is a one-sided conversation. Shaken by the violence of it, he promised himself he would never resort to such cowardice. Thereafter, the few times he himself had made the decision to end a relationship, he had always done so face to face, even if it meant enduring a difficult conversation.

So the telephone rang at the Hills' flat. It was a production assistant, suggesting a meeting. Both father and son tried to conceal their excitement. It was a good sign, they both thought, never imagining that David felt he should always be there to deliver bad news. To him, it was a principle of courtesy and a way of softening the blow of disappointment. Not for one moment did David think that this invitation would increase the expectations of the boy about to be rejected. It happens; in trying to be sensitive, we end up making it worse. But the misunderstanding wouldn't last for long. As soon as Martin saw the producer's face, he knew it was not Harry Potter who was about to sit down on the office sofa. David's face was grave, and you could already see in his eyes the speech to come. But the words had to be said out loud, the words that Martin would never forget.

'It's not him, is it?' asked John, anxiously.

'Listen, this isn't easy. I wanted to see you both . . . I wanted to see you, Martin . . . I didn't want to tell you over the phone. I know it won't be easy to hear what I'm about to say.'

'. . .'

'This was a painful decision for us too, because everyone thought you were fantastic, and blessed with a rare talent. And by the way, you can count on me in your future career. I'm sure we can work together on other projects. But as you've guessed, we aren't going to hire you to play Harry . . .'

Martin could no longer hear the producer's words. His head had turned hot and fuzzy. He felt as though he were falling while sitting down. He had of course prepared for this possible failure, but the impact of its reality was brutal. He didn't feel capable of withstanding such a shock. As the years pass, little by little we learn how to endure life's blows. Human life can perhaps be summarised as a constant trial through disillusionment, which culminates in a successful, or unsuccessful, way of managing pain. But at the time, Martin was just eleven years old. It was insurmountable. The promise of a marvellous adventure had just been ripped away from him.

John wanted to get up and take his son in his arms, but he sat and listened to the producer. Frozen, he continued to observe the etiquette of the meeting, although he now found it absurd. What good could come from listening to these empty words? It was over. Why had David sought out his son, given him so much hope, only to then reject him? They hadn't asked for any of this. John's mind then alighted on a terrible thought: 'Have I passed the curse of failure on to my son?' And then: 'The rotten apple doesn't fall far from the tree.' It was all linked, of course it was. For years now, he had been humiliated by his own existence, and now it was his son's turn. He was spending his life being mistreated by miniature dictators on film sets. As for his inventions – forget it. Everyone thought his umbrella-tie was a joke. And then there was Jeanne. She had moved countries just to be sure she wouldn't run into him. How could he possibly have fathered a son able to spark the excitement of the whole world?

John continued his disparaging internal monologue for a while. It was absurd: he had done everything he could to help his son prepare for failure, and it was surely also thanks to him in part that Martin had performed so well. David was still singing Martin's praises, too. But, whatever – they had chosen the Other. All these compliments were nothing but a sticking plaster. The producer still wanted to offer him something.

'Unfortunately, all the major roles have been cast, but you could be part of one of the bigger scenes. Like the ones in the Hogwarts Great Hall—'

'An extra,' Martin cut him off quietly.

'Yes . . . Well, no. We could arrange for you to have a line or two,' David added feebly.

'Thanks, but I don't really want that,' whispered Martin, his voice extinguished by his shattered dream.

David was embarrassed at having made this suggestion. In trying to soften the blow for Martin, he had offered him a drop of water when he needed an ocean. But there was no other choice. For a moment, he thought of making him a promise: they would write him a role in the second instalment of the series. But he changed his mind. It would be best not to get the boy's hopes up, in case he had to dash them once again. But how to console him? There was another option, but it was even more humiliating. He couldn't ask him to be Daniel Radcliffe's body double. The filming would be so gruelling that the main actors would need help for certain action scenes, for lighting tests or rear views. No, no – it was out of the question to mention that.

The Story of David Holmes

A few months later, the production team would discover a rare gem: the young sportsman chosen to form part of the Quidditch team in the two first instalments of the series. Due to his physical prowess, they had offered him the chance to be Daniel Radcliffe's stunt double for all his action scenes. He would also have to coach Daniel several times a week. It was the beginning of a friendship between the two young men. But in January 2009, during the shooting of the penultimate film in the series, *Harry Potter and the Deathly Hallows: Part I*, David's life would change irrevocably. During the stunt, the young wizard had to zigzag through balls of fire on a broomstick. It was during rehearsals for this dangerous scene that the accident happened. The cable that David was attached to had given way, throwing him violently against a wall. When he fell to the ground, he knew something awful had happened. He couldn't move. He was transferred to Watford Hospital, close to the studios. His spinal cord was damaged; they told him he would be paralysed for life. He was just twenty-five years old.

There was nothing more to say: it was over, and it was best to admit it. John and Martin thanked the producer for his kindness, in spite of everything. They stood motionless outside the building for a moment.

'You have to look at the positives—'

'Positives? What positives?'

'It was a heck of an experience anyway.'

'That doesn't mean anything, at the end of the day.'

'I know.'

'. . .'

'The good news is that you've found your calling,' John continued.

'. . .'

'It's true! You're so talented, kiddo, everyone said it. I spotted a drama class close to home.'

'. . .'

'And we can always invite the producer along if you're in a show, and I have some good connections in that world, you know—'

'No.'

'What do you mean, no?'

'I don't want to do any more acting. That's all finished.'

'You're just saying that now because you're disappointed, of course. But I saw how much you loved it—'

'No, Dad. I'm not doing any more acting.' Martin cut him off with such conviction in his voice that it brooked no argument. The feeling of being wanted and then rejected – he never wanted to experience that again.

30

That evening, the house was silent. John had let Jeanne know, but Martin didn't want to speak to her. He didn't want to spend any more time talking about his feelings; he wished to put an end to his unhappiness. His feelings were easy enough to guess: he wanted now to forget all about it, not talk about it any more. The subject became taboo.

That first night, Martin couldn't stop replaying the audition. Which was the moment that had ruined it? What could he have done better? It wouldn't change anything anyway. Life doesn't have a rewind button. He had missed his chance, and now had to face the future in the wake of this disaster. Of course, he couldn't take all the responsibility. The other actor had surely been better. And there was nothing he could do about that. It was fate. All he could do was curse the destiny that had thrown the Other in his path. So often, there is someone who can take our place, who blocks our way. It had happened to him before, at school, and at the sports club; occasions when he had almost come first until the appearance of someone who performed better than him. Is it always this way? Every person's life is, at one moment or another, ruined by another person's life.

The image of the Other haunted him. He must be celebrating his victory, intoxicated by the life that awaited him. Martin felt a bottomless jealousy invading his body. 'Why him and not me?' he repeated over and over, like the chorus in the song of his bitterness. In the fever of that disappointment-laden night, he wondered: 'What if I got rid of him?' A crazy idea – absurd, demented. But if one person is ruining your life, surely you just need to remove them from the picture? He remembered a story everyone had been talking about a few years previously. An American figure skater, unable to accept coming second, had hired someone to injure her opponent's knees. But she was quickly found out. If the other actor were assassinated, the police would probably come looking for him immediately. In the maze of his morbid thoughts, he imagined himself in prison. His mind was really wandering. It was ridiculous. In the end he fell asleep, completely lost.

PART TWO

1

As the months passed, Martin's disappointment faded. He even managed to stop thinking about his failure, or at least managed to think about it without his heart breaking. But he preferred it when nobody spoke about it at all, not wishing to open old wounds. Of course, he heard people talking about the book here and there at school, but he simply distanced himself from those conversations. It was easy enough to avoid the worst of that sad memory.

It was in November of 2001 that his life was turned upside down. Strangely, Martin hadn't foreseen the inevitable – nor had his parents, for that matter. Yet it seemed rather obvious that the adaptation of the phenomenon that was *Harry Potter* wouldn't pass unnoticed. It was worse than that. The previews of the film immediately provoked a kind of collective never-before-seen hysteria. The day of its release, 16 November, *Harry Potter* was all anybody could talk about. Martin's torment began in earnest. From that moment on, it would be impossible for him to escape his failure. He couldn't claim that famous 'right to be forgotten' that criminals can invoke. Worse still, it seemed that the entire country was rubbing his nose in it. You couldn't turn on the television without seeing Daniel Radcliffe's radiant expression, without hearing about the wonders of his day-to-day life. His face was plastered all over London. Everyone thought he was brilliant; they wanted to know everything about him. Apparently, he would soon be meeting the Queen. The life of the Other would forever be on display.

There seemed to be no way out. Every part of his life had been infiltrated. Even his English teacher had been swept up in the hysteria, devoting an entire lesson to the vocabulary of

Harry Potter. Like a penance, Martin had to learn the meaning of all the words J. K. Rowling had invented. At least he could escape to Paris at weekends – but his respite was short-lived. In December, France too would fall for the film that would sell more than ten million tickets: an extraordinary number. And it would be like that all over the world. Soon, there would be no corner of the planet which wouldn't remind him of this erasing of his destiny.

Seeing his son so withdrawn, John began to worry. He too felt harassed by the omnipresence of *Harry Potter*. He urged Martin to talk about it; it was the only way to shake off this feeling of suffocation. For the first time, Martin tried to put his feelings into words. To him, it was like being dumped by a girl and then having to see her every day. But no – that romantic comparison didn't seem strong enough to him. It was much worse than that. 'Everything constantly reminds me of my failure. It's awful,' he said eventually. John, shaken by his son's sadness, didn't know what to do. In a horrible way, it made him think of another similar destiny.

The Story of Pete Best

He was nicknamed 'the unluckiest man in the world'. He had been kicked out of the Beatles just a few weeks before they became the most successful band of all time. A friend of John, Paul and George's from Liverpool, he had joined the line-up of the band during their long stay in Hamburg. Pete always remained at a distance, a loner. The others thought him overconfident and haughty. Worse still: he was good-looking and all the women fancied him, which got on the others' nerves. In August 1962, an article announced the band's signing by EMI, accompanied by a photo of . . . Pete Best. So perhaps it was just a question of jealousy, but when the producer expressed doubts about the drummer's abilities, they replaced him without the slightest hesitation – without even having the decency to tell him to his face. They never spoke again. That's how Ringo Starr became part of the legend. The Beatles became an unparalleled phenomenon, provoking hysteria wherever they went. In Liverpool, everyone knew Pete as a member of the band; he couldn't now step outside without receiving pitying looks. While his former bandmates became rich and famous, he remained on the sidelines like a pariah. His failure was worse than any other, because the whole world knew about it. All his life, he would constantly be confronted with what he had missed out on. You couldn't turn on the television, listen to the radio or open a magazine without coming across references to *A Hard Day's Night*. His life became a living hell, to the point where he attempted suicide in 1965. He slowly got back on his feet, but he decided to stop playing music. He didn't want anyone to come and listen to him out of morbid curiosity. While he struggled, his old bandmates – now multimillionaires – didn't come to his aid. Eventually, as time went on, he became a baker. But he would never escape the curse. In the eyes of the world, he would always be the man who had almost been a Beatle.

It was only natural that John drew this comparison – this idea of being constantly confronted with the life you could have had. But there was one major difference. Unlike Pete Best, Martin was a nobody. If he could manage to escape the memory of his failure, he could get through this. Of course, this escape would be difficult. There would always be a new film or a new book. J. K. Rowling had announced seven volumes; it wasn't even close to being over. From that moment on, Martin would have to try and lead his life sheltered from the famous wizard. He no longer went to the cinema, for fear of seeing a trailer for the film, and didn't dare turn on the television. He also cut himself off from his friends, unable to bear all the conversations which inevitably led to *Harry Potter*. Every person seeks the cure for their suffering as best they can. Luckily, he had never told his friends about the audition. He was relieved that he hadn't done so, that they wouldn't now ask him to recount his misfortune at every turn. His disappointment at least had the merit of remaining secret.

2

Martin was about to be confronted with another tragedy. In fact, perhaps the two were linked. Yes, thinking about it, it seemed obvious to him that his father had started coughing just after his failed audition. A mild cough to begin with, which soon became more and more worrying. John made an appointment with the GP, who referred him to a lung specialist. It is never a good sign when a doctor hands you over to a colleague. But John went to the appointment without any particular apprehension. He had never considered illness a possibility, proceeding as always without worrying about the worst-case scenario – in matters of health, at least. The examination took longer than anticipated. The doctor was struggling to find the right words, which said it all. The cancer had already spread; it couldn't be stopped. It was in his lungs. He who had never smoked. Absurdity upon absurdity. All his life, John had been out of step; never in the right place. At the Cure concert, in his professional life, when he met David Heyman. And now he found himself with an illness that was going to do him so much harm.

When the sentence was delivered, John said nothing. He was the type who thought that things only existed if you named them. Perhaps he could be cured by injecting doses of secrecy. In truth, he didn't want people to reduce him to just his illness. When a person announces they have cancer, cancer is all you can see in them. The doctor had not been optimistic: six to eight months at most. After a few weeks, John felt as though his body was burning. He had to take sick leave. On his last day at work, he walked away from the set without saying a word to anyone. He left the filming of *Love Actually*, a perfect romantic comedy, behind him: he was out of step one last time.

Soon, John could no longer look after Martin. His son would grow up without him: an unbearable thought. There was no choice but to call Jeanne and let her know. For a moment, he imagined that she would return to be by his side; even if it was out of pity, it would still suit him. She was in shock at his announcement, and stammered a few words before trying to be practical.

'But you could get better, with treatment . . .'

'It's too late.'

John began to cry softly down the phone. In finally sharing the awful truth, he felt as though his insides were collapsing. They had to talk about Martin, about the arrangements to come. Jeanne couldn't take him to Paris and separate him from his father. It was up to her to move. It would take her a few days to get organised, but yes, she would return to London. She tried to find words of comfort, while holding back her own sobs.

3

Martin had noticed that his father seemed to become breathless quickly, that he was coughing a lot, but John kept telling him: 'Everything is fine.' Why wouldn't he believe him? However, when he learned his mother would soon be returning to look after him, he was forced to conclude that the situation was indeed worrying. But John continued to minimise the seriousness of his condition. He told Martin he was just going through a rough patch, 'one of life's tests'. He was like an actor on a cardboard-cut-out set. Everything sounded false, but Martin pretended to believe him. After all, perhaps fiction could triumph over reality.

While they were doing their shopping at Night and Delhi, the Indian grocer's on the corner of the street, John had a dizzy spell. Martin saw his father suddenly fall to the ground before his eyes. He would never forget that image. He immediately associated the sight with that of the Twin Towers in New York, destroyed by terrorists a few months earlier. Afterwards, he would be unable to explain why he had linked the two events – one personal, one universal – like this. Yet it was the same image, that of a fall that seemed unimaginable. Martin rushed towards his father. John, still conscious, tried to smile; a smile to keep up appearances. It was time to stop pretending that everything was fine. But a moment earlier, there had still been an illusion they could hold on to. They were wandering through the aisles, and John had said to his son: 'Don't forget to get those yoghurts you like.' It was the last thing he had said before falling, the last utterance of normal life.

Martin held his father's hand. The shopkeeper, whom they knew well, had brought him a glass of water, before realising that wouldn't be enough; he needed to call an ambulance. The customers crowded around the man on the floor, hovering somewhere between voyeurism and compassion. A woman took his pulse, saying she was a doctor, but after that said nothing more. She gave Martin a fleeting look, then ruffled his hair. She asked him which school he went to, and Martin answered politely. A few minutes later, an ambulance parked outside the shop. Two paramedics got out and hurried towards John. They asked him a few questions; his replies were barely audible. They could just hear him gasping weakly: 'My son . . .' One of the paramedics turned towards Martin and asked, 'Is this your dad?' He nodded, and the man suggested they move to one side to chat. The boy didn't want to leave his father, but the paramedic reassured him.

'Look, my colleague is going to take good care of him. He's very nice.'

'. . .'

'We'll just be over here. Everything is going to be fine.'

He produced one reassuring phrase after another, before moving on to the next step. 'We're going to take your dad with us to do some tests. Just some checks, it's nothing serious. Is there someone who can come and pick you up?'

'I don't know.'

'Where's your mum?'

'In Paris.'

'Right, okay. Is there someone else in your family who could come?'

'No, we don't have anyone here.'

'What about a school friend? We could call their parents?'

'I don't know . . .'

The logistical questions went on for a while before reaching an impasse. Martin would never forget this feeling, either – of having nowhere to go, of sensing that no one knew what to do with him. In the end he gave them his old babysitter's name, Rose. When they took his father away, he wanted to follow him to the hospital, but they refused. A child couldn't be left in a corridor or a waiting room. He insisted, and they had to restrain him by force.

So Martin stayed in the shop, with the woman who had taken his father's pulse. The shopkeeper offered him some sweets. The adults didn't know what to do while they were waiting. Rose eventually arrived, out of breath, and took Martin in her arms. He's so grown up, he's a teenager now, she thought, suddenly embarrassed by her spontaneous gesture. They would have a lovely evening, like in the old days, she reassured him. But nothing would ever be like the old days again. Why was no one talking to him normally? Why were they telling him it wasn't serious? Why were they talking about having a lovely evening when his father was going to die? Just before he left the shop, Martin went to the yoghurt aisle to pick up his favourite brand. The adults thought this was his way of trying to quietly reclaim a bit of normality – but he was just obeying his father's last instruction. The shopkeeper gave him the yoghurts for free, and Martin left with Rose. On the way home, she tried to talk about other things, asking him about the latest goings-on at school, eventually resorting to the subject of the endless overcast weather. Martin remained silent. He kept seeing his father falling, over and over again; the image played on a loop inside his head. As soon as they got home, he called his mother, who said she would take the first Eurostar the next morning. She spoke to Rose too, giving her some inessential instructions, to mask the feeling of being so horribly far away.

Throughout the evening, Martin phoned the hospital several times, and was consistently told that his father was under observation. So this was what being ill was like: being observed. Rose suggested they watch cartoons, or play Monopoly, 'like the old days', but Martin wanted to go to bed. Something was bothering him, and he wanted to cut the evening short. Two years earlier, he had explained to his father that now he was old enough, he didn't need a babysitter. The truth was something else entirely. He wanted to distance himself from all contaminated memories; for him, Rose was linked to the audition. Without her hasty departure, none of it would have happened. Martin wanted someone to blame for his misfortune.

4

The next morning, Jeanne arrived in London. She hadn't been back since the separation. As she left the station, she was bombarded with dozens of images, as though her memories had been patiently waiting at the border. As soon as she had dropped her things off at the flat, she went to the hospital. The news was not good. In the hospital room, she took the hand of the man who had once been her husband, and he thought: 'So, the only way I can see the woman I love again is by dying.'

At the end of the afternoon, Jeanne waited for her son at the school gate. She realised how much she had missed this. She and Martin had had a wonderful time together, but a huge part of his life had completely passed her by. She felt unsettled only spending Saturdays and Sundays with her son. When she spotted him, she signalled to him with an almost imperceptible wave of the hand, as though she was afraid of disturbing him. When he saw her, he forgot the tragic context for a moment and his heart leapt with pride: his mother had come to pick him up.

That evening, after kissing Martin goodnight, Jeanne sat in

the living room for a long time. In the half-light, she looked back on the scenes of her old married life. She could remember everything about their first night in this flat; she could still see the piles of boxes, the same boxes that would soon need to be packed again. Although their last few years had been difficult for her, happy images came flooding back. Everything was there, so vivid. She could see John sitting on the living-room floor surrounded by dozens of sketches, muttering instructions for the creation of some machine that would never see the light of day. Jeanne whispered to him how much she had loved him.

Her train of thought led to Marc, the man who had touched her back. After his long, assiduous campaign of seduction, she had finally given in. But after the chaotic end to her marriage, and the painful affair, Jeanne didn't really feel ready to consider a new relationship. Her professional life fulfilled her; she wanted to go away on reporting trips without having to answer to anyone. But she had changed her mind, just when Marc had started to give up. By backing off, Marc had become more attractive to her: the strange workings of desire. And there was something else: Jeanne was thirty-five, and was wondering if she wanted to have another child. Anything was possible.

She spent a moment mulling over the possibilities, painting her future in the frame of her past. In the end she fell asleep on the sofa. That night, and the ones that would follow. Every day, the news would get worse.

5

Only a few weeks later, John's losing battle was over. The day of the funeral, Jeanne was overcome with deep emotion. It was the same cemetery where she had first fallen in love with John. It was where they had taken their first walk, that lovely walk to honour the pact John had made with his grandmother. And now it was all over. If all existence is a struggle, it was only more so among the echoes of this setting. She felt as though their life together had lasted for no more than a few scenes. Laughter, tears, excitement, boredom; and a child. Martin was here right beside her, so incredibly stoic. His beloved father had been ripped away from him. The violence of this event was made even worse by just how few people were present. John had lived a hermit's life, barely forming any real friendships. Jeanne had called a priest, even though no one in the family was Catholic. She just wanted someone there to say a few words, if only to fill the silence. But there was nothing to say. John dying of cancer before he'd even reached forty – it was hard to know what to say. Mercifully, it began to rain. The scene became blurred by the falling rain, as though to distract from the tragedy. For days now, Martin had been absorbed in his father's files. He had found a large piece of fabric criss-crossed with wire – the famous umbrella-tie. He had decided to wear it as a tribute, even if it seemed impractical to have this mass of fabric around his neck. But now it was raining, he could open it above his head. The rain continued to pour down his face, but he was proud to honour his father's memory in this way.

So as not to add a house move to an already difficult time, Jeanne decided to stay in London until the end of the school year. She could keep working, writing articles on British current affairs. Marc called her often, but she cut these conversations short. Her son was her first priority; she was worried. She felt as though in burying his father, he had also buried his childhood. It was as though he had been shoved in the back, forced into adulthood before his time. Martin didn't dare tell his mother, but his real unhappiness was of a different sort, and he wasn't proud of it. On cinema screens, *Harry Potter and the Chamber of Secrets*, the second instalment of the film series, was again breaking all records. Enthusiasm for it could have dried up, as sometimes happens with sequels, but no – it had increased. Every day, thousands of new fans joined the fray. Panicked by this latest onslaught, Martin retreated even further into himself. At school, they blamed the change in his demeanour on recent events, and teachers whispered, 'That's the boy who's lost his father,' as he walked past. Those words intensified his dread. A boy who'd lost his father – like Harry Potter.

Eventually, Jeanne understood that her son's gloominess was linked, at least in part, to the failed audition. She could see the mood he sank into when the subject was even remotely alluded to. She understood his bitterness of course, but she couldn't have imagined the intensity of his angst. In any case, she decided he needed to talk to someone neutral. Jeanne made an appointment with Dr Xenakis, who worked locally. Martin welcomed this decision. Perhaps this doctor could remove the weight that was crushing his soul. When he met him, Martin wasn't surprised; the child psychiatrist looked exactly how he had imagined. With his pronounced Greek accent and his face covered in wrinkles, he was like the incarnation of an ancient sage.

'Your mother is worried about you,' Xenakis began. 'She thinks you need to talk to someone. What do you think?'

'I think it might do me good.'

'I hope so. How old are you?'

'Thirteen.'

'Not an easy age. There are so many changes, at all stages of life. And certainly, it's been more difficult for you than for others. Do you want to talk to me about your dad?'

'There's not much to say.'

'Can you try and explain what it is you're feeling? Your mother tells me she thinks you're more withdrawn than before. Sometimes, when we lose someone close to us, we feel a deep anger. And that's normal. We feel the world is unfair—'

'Yeah, it is unfair. But . . .'

'What?'

'. . .'

'Martin, you know you can talk to me. Everything will stay between us.'

'I feel like my life is ruined,' Martin blurted out suddenly.

Xenakis paused, taken aback. This painful admission was, to say the least, unexpected at this early stage in the conversation. To temper the harshness of Martin's words, he tried to qualify them:

'Martin, at your age, there's nothing that suggests that. You have your whole life ahead of you.'

'. . .'

'Do you want to tell me why you feel this way?'

Martin briefly debated whether or not to tell him everything, but decided to stay quiet. Just like with his friends, he couldn't stand the idea of someone knowing that he had almost become Harry Potter. Cornered, he murmured a few vague words about a recent failure.

'Was this with a girl?' Xenakis asked.

'No.'

'Or a boy?'

'No, it's not that.'

'Well, I don't want to force you to talk about it. Often we

feel like we cannot overcome a failure. But if you want to hear my opinion, I'll tell you what I think: all failures can be turned into something positive.'

'. . .'

'I don't know what is causing your pain, but I'm sure that one day you will realise that this pain can also be your greatest strength, in helping you to achieve whatever you put your mind to.'

Martin found this statement ridiculous. He didn't see how the humiliation he had lived through could be transformed into any kind of strength. On the contrary, he was convinced that he could no longer trust Xenakis. Despite his good intentions, the doctor couldn't do anything for him. The only solution would be to go back in time and start the audition over again. It wasn't a child psychiatrist he needed, but a magician; it was Dumbledore he needed to consult to make him better. While Martin's mind wandered, Xenakis continued to list the benefits of failure. He mentioned Steve Jobs's journey (perhaps he thought of him because he went past the huge Apple Store on Regent Street every morning). Full of himself, puffed up with arrogance, he had eventually been fired from Apple, the business he himself had founded. And in the end, it was thanks to this hammer blow that he had matured, and returned armed with the strength of humility. He had gone on to create iMacs, a new generation of computers, and invented the slogan THINK DIFFERENT.

'Are you listening to me?'

'Yeah.'

'I don't know what you make of that example, but I think it's a good lesson in moving forward. He became a better man because of his failure. Our lives aren't ruined; we just start over.'

To compensate for his patient's silence, Xenakis decided to

mention other stories that might be inspiring for him. He went on:

'Another example that I really like is J. K. Rowling. She was on benefits, desperate – her life was nothing but a series of failures. And look what she's accomplished! I imagine you've read *Harry Potter*, like everyone else.'

'. . .'

'Hmm, Martin? Have you read it?'

'. . .'

'Are you all right?' Xenakis asked, noticing Martin had suddenly turned pale.

Martin was in shock. For a brief moment, he really thought he was the victim of a conspiracy. The world wanted to belittle him further, to humiliate him. He managed to snap out of it and regain his composure. Even here, in this supposed safe place, they still talked, they always talked about that bloody book. As the psychiatrist continued to ask him what was going on, Martin stood up and left the office without another word to the doctor. Xenakis was stunned. In thirty years of practice, he had never had a session end like that before. He would try to meet Martin again, but it was in vain. He tried, too, to get an explanation from his mother, but she only repeated her son's words: 'He doesn't want to see you again.' The experience would remain a mystery to him, a puzzling riddle. What could he have done wrong?

7

Martin became even more withdrawn. His mother didn't know what to do. She had tried to take his mind off things, but it wasn't easy. You can't take your mind off something in the way you can take a coat off. Thankfully, the school year was coming to an end, and they would be leaving England. A change of scenery could only be positive. At the start of the summer, Martin spent his days sorting through his childhood toys, packing them into boxes, before deciding to throw them all away. When it came to a beloved cuddly toy, his mother asked him: 'Are you sure? You should really keep it.' He shook his head. He felt he should put the happiness of his childhood days behind him; he didn't want to arrive in Paris with London in his suitcases. At the end of July, they boarded the Eurostar with one-way tickets. During the journey, Jeanne suggested they get a snack from the buffet carriage, but Martin refused, saying he wasn't hungry. Eating anything other than his father's sandwiches would have been like betraying him. Three hours later, when they arrived at Gare du Nord, he announced: 'From now on, we'll speak only French.'

8

Jeanne had planned to take her son to the USA for the month of August; he had always talked excitedly about New York. But the moment she mentioned the idea, he seemed reluctant. Truthfully, he was afraid of going to a country known for its first-rate *Harry Potter* merchandise. As a diversion, he announced: 'My dream is to go to Greenland.' Clearly, Jeanne no longer understood her son, but she wanted to make him happy at all costs. She began to make enquiries, preparing for the trip, and came across an article which named Greenland 'the island of despair'. It said: 'One in five inhabitants has had suicidal thoughts.' Not the best destination, then, to try and reignite Martin's will to live. But Martin seemed truly excited at the idea of the expedition, so Jeanne consented to leave for somewhere freezing, in the middle of August. On an outing, they found themselves alone in the midst of an immense whiteness. Martin said softly, 'Thank you, Maman.' She had given him just what he had been looking for: a place on earth with no human presence.

9

Martin enrolled in Year 9 at Lamartine School. Although he was sociable enough, he nonetheless avoided forming any ties. If another pupil ventured a little too close to his private realm, Martin found all kinds of excuses to step back – an attitude he also adopted during another awkward moment. In the canteen, a girl approached him and said: 'It's crazy how much you look like the Harry Potter actor!' He didn't know how to respond. The girl thought he was weird. But it was only to be expected: of course almost getting the part meant that he looked like Daniel Radcliffe. So he decided to cut his hair shorter, having already abandoned the round glasses some time ago. He was like a man being hunted by the police, changing his appearance to avoid being found.

Seeing Martin alone so often, his mother began to worry, and suggested: 'What if we threw a party on Saturday?' And another time: 'Don't you want to invite a friend over?' He refused every time, without seeming unhappy. It's just his way, she told herself for a while, thinking perhaps he had inherited it from his father. But she quickly changed her mind. As a small child, he had never been like this. He had spent his time playing in the park with his friends and loved having sleepovers at their houses. In the end, she confronted him.

'Are you still thinking about the casting?'

'I don't want to talk about it, Maman.'

'I know. But you can tell me anything. I have to be honest. It's not normal to be so solitary at your age.'

'I don't feel comfortable around other people.'

'But why not?'

'I can't help it. I'm always afraid that they'll mention . . . you know what. And that it will upset me.'

'But, my darling, there will always be people talking about it. You simply can't avoid it.'

'. . .'

Martin did not respond. He knew his mother was right. Not only did he feel he had ruined his life, as he had confessed to Xenakis, but that he had to go on living in a hostile world. For the time being, he saw no other solution than to protect himself with solitude. Jeanne realised the situation was worse than she thought. She told herself she needed to bring some life back into their lives.

10

Up until now, Jeanne hadn't wanted to impose her new partner on her son. She thought, 'He's just lost his father, he needs time' – a point of view that Marc found absurd. Since Jeanne's stay in London he was tired of making do with a stolen hour together here or there. Behind his understanding façade, he felt it wasn't good for a child to be mollycoddled. He himself had a son, Hugo, whom he saw very little of at the moment – he had lost custody of him. Jeanne couldn't work out what had really happened there. She only knew one side of the story: 'My ex-wife is a bitch. She lied about all kinds of things just to get my money. But it won't last. According to my lawyer,

I'll get my son back after the next hearing.' Jeanne found it hard to square these words with the gentle man she knew and loved. When he spoke about his old life, it was always venomously.

Jeanne decided to let Marc move in. She realised immediately that she had been wrong to worry. He spent his first night in the apartment, and from the moment they woke up in the morning, it was as if he had always been there. Even Martin seemed to appreciate this breath of fresh air. The one-to-one conversations with his mother were sometimes intense. As for Marc, he behaved more naturally than he had at their first meeting. He no longer tried to forge a relationship at any cost, by talking about things he knew nothing about. In short, he had abandoned the subject of football. He looked at Martin and sighed, 'You remind me of my son.' He missed Hugo so much that he saw reflections of him in all other children. Nothing is more visible than absence. Thankfully, in due course Marc managed to gain custody of his son every other week, and the four of them began to spend time together. Without having planned it, the couple who had been piecing together their relationship like a dot-to-dot had become a blended family. The two boys got on marvellously – nobody could have predicted what was to come.

11

A few months later, they decided to move into a bigger apartment together. Every other week, Martin found himself without Hugo, so his life was divided into two parts. On the evenings when his mother went out with Marc, he wandered in a silent realm where, the night before, there had been joyful chaos. Modern childhoods often have this bipolar atmosphere.

Jeanne and Martin regularly went out for dinner one-on-one. It was important to preserve these moments when it was 'just the two of them'. She used these occasions to probe him, to try and find out how he was. Every time she broached the subject of Harry Potter, he dodged it. But the situation wasn't improving; he continued to avoid having any social life, deeming it dangerous. One evening, Jeanne mentioned her relationship with her own parents – a rare event. Martin knew almost nothing about his mother's childhood. He had only heard her speak of a cold middle-class background. She had left for London to escape that hostile environment. Her parents hadn't even come to the wedding, believing – without even knowing John – that she was making a monumental error in marrying a 'nobody'. She had never seen them again.

'Doesn't that make you feel sad?' asked Martin.

'No, I decided not to let it affect me. I think we can achieve that in life. We can overcome things that do us harm.'

So that was her point. She had spoken of her pain so she could draw from it a lesson for her son: 'We can overcome things that do us harm.' But the situations weren't comparable. Jeanne had cut her ties with her parents, yes. But how would she have handled seeing their faces on posters everywhere? How could she have withstood constantly seeing her mother's face whenever she turned on the television? Could she conceive of a world where everyone's favourite topic of conversation was her parents? Imagine for a moment that the cause of your suffering received the same media attention as Harry Potter. Overcoming things that do us harm would become a little more complicated.

After this admission, Jeanne announced: 'I told Marc about the audition.'

'Really? Why? You know very well that I don't want anyone to know.'

'I know, I'm sorry. It just slipped out during conversation. I was worried about you, and Marc asked me what was wrong. He's concerned about you. You know how much he loves you.'

'. . .'

'In any case, he could see very well how difficult this must be for you.'

'. . .'

'Marc really is a good person.'

Martin didn't doubt it, but for the first time, he felt his mother had betrayed him. She hadn't meant him any harm, of course, but her betrayal forced him to reconsider their relationship.

12

Harry Potter and the Order of the Phoenix, the fifth book in the series, was about to hit France. On 3 December 2003, to be precise. That day, or rather the night before, fans queued for hours. Bookshops opened at the stroke of midnight to make the moment even more of an event. Year after year, the phenomenon had grown monstrously. In the UK, the book had sold almost two million copies in just one day. Unheard of – unimaginable, even. For the first time, a book in English had stayed the whole summer on the bestseller list in France; readers who could manage without the translation had already flocked to buy the book. J. K. Rowling had become the most read author in the world.

Martin particularly dreaded times like this when it was impossible for him to avoid it. Since his impassioned reading of the first book, he hadn't opened a *Harry Potter* book. He knew that all around him people were devouring the new story.

They were bound to ask his opinion, and he would have to admit he hadn't read it, trying to appear aloof. But the torment wouldn't end there. They would try to convince him, encourage him, make him feel guilty. 'What? You haven't read it? Impossible! I'll lend it to you.' They would constantly trigger his worst nightmare. Of course, there was an upside: the publication of the books hurt less than the film releases. There was a sort of hierarchy of pain.

One day, when he was once again being implored to read the latest *Harry Potter*, he thought about replying: 'I can't. It's too painful for me.' They surely would have asked him why. And Martin would have launched into his incredible story. So many times, the confession had been on the tip of his tongue. To begin with, no one would believe him. But, with proof, he would quickly convince them. What would happen then? Would they make fun of his failure? Surely not. He was convinced of the opposite: that the account of his wretched adventure would have lent him an air of mystery. Everyone would crowd around to question him. They would beg him for behind-the-scenes stories. And if he mentioned his meeting with Ron and Hermione, he would become the star of the school, without a doubt. So why? Why didn't he tell them? For the simple reason that he didn't want to be associated with this failure. He didn't want to read it in people's eyes for evermore: 'Oh, that's the boy who was almost Harry Potter.'

13

After *L'Événement du jeudi* closed down, Jeanne had a string of freelance jobs before joining the international politics team at *Le Point*. She found herself authorised to follow the presidential delegation at international summits. Over the next few months, she would travel to the States on numerous occasions to cover the presidential campaign, and the battle between George W. Bush and his Democrat opponent, John Kerry. She even obtained an interview with the latter. She felt at ease in the heart of this new team, and thrived on the pressure of the Monday meetings. During the last meeting, Marie-Françoise Leclère had announced that she was negotiating with Gallimard Jeunesse for an exclusive interview with J. K. Rowling. 'It's not confirmed yet,' she clarified. 'But if I get it, it will be her only interview.' Everyone was excited about the potential scoop.

Jeanne couldn't stop mulling over this information for the rest of the meeting. Nothing else interested her. She thought: J. K. Rowling is right there, so close, so accessible. What if this is the solution to make my son feel better? As she left the meeting room, she walked up to Marie-Françoise.

'Congratulations on the Rowling piece, that's great.'

'Oh, nothing's final yet.'

'You know, I was the first person to write about her in France.'

'Really? I didn't know that.'

'Yes, I'm a huge fan of hers. Actually, I wanted to ask you—'

'What?'

'If you do land that interview, I'd love to be the one to do it.'

'You? Are you trying to steal my job? Should I interview Angela Merkel for you?' Marie-Françoise replied with a big smile.

In the end, Marie-Françoise suggested they both go together: 'That way, you can ask her what she thinks about the situation in Iraq . . .' Any opinion J. K. Rowling had on any subject was of interest. Jeanne thanked her colleague profusely for the kind offer and returned to her office. Once she was alone, she let herself get excited about it. She could tell the celebrated author about Martin; she must remember him. But would the author agree to meet him? Surely she would – people were always praising her humanity and her altruism. Since the world had learned of her success, and her riches, too, it was said that every day she received hundreds of letters from people begging her for help. It must be suffocating, thought Jeanne. The dark side of success. The constant weight of others' suffering. Helping a single mother and her disabled son; finding work for someone unemployed, or a house for someone homeless; financing a heart operation or a kidney transplant. There were also less gloomy entreaties, such as marriage proposals or requests to pull strings to get a book published. Like the Pope, receiving grievances was her daily reality. Surely she would find the words to help Martin. But did these words even exist? Maybe this meeting would only conjure up the alternative-reality scenario of J. K. Rowling's own ruined life: if nobody had wanted *Harry Potter*, what would have become of her?

Jeanne knew that interviews with the bestselling author were planned to the nth degree, and carefully controlled. She couldn't tell her Martin's story, especially not in front of another journalist. The best thing to do would be to give the author a letter with her contact details. Yes, that was what she needed to do, and then try to see her again. For a moment, she wondered whether Martin would appreciate her idea. Meeting J. K. Rowling certainly wouldn't change the course of his life. And he hated talking about the subject. What should she do? She was at a loss. Jeanne went back and forth between the two possibilities for a few days, but to no avail. In the end, however, J. K. Rowling decided not to come to Paris to promote her book: there would be no interview.

14

Christmas came, and the blended family enjoyed a traditional Christmas Eve feast. It was the first time they had celebrated the holiday together. For Martin, it was the second Christmas without his father. It upset him that day; it would upset him always.

That said, the evening was a success. The two boys had a good time together, even if Hugo displayed the immaturity often characteristic of spoiled children. Since his father had regained custody, Hugo had become a little tyrant. The two adults had a tacit agreement not to interfere in the upbringing of each other's children, but sometimes Jeanne couldn't stop herself from saying: 'You let Hugo get away with everything, it's not good.'

Her partner listened to her, of course – she was probably right, he thought – but it was impossible for him to act otherwise. 'I know, I know,' he replied. 'But it's been hard for the poor kid.' Hugo sometimes abused the power he had over his father, happily exerting his tyranny over him. But for the most part, everyone got along well enough, so it didn't escalate.

At midnight, they opened their presents. Jeanne had given the two boys the same thing: an iPod. It was the easiest way to avoid comparisons and rivalries. They jumped for joy and began discussing their favourite songs. But there were other parcels. Martin saw his name on one of them and hurried to unwrap it. He turned white; as did Jeanne, who realised at once the mistake that had been made. She immediately looked at the guilty party.

'But . . . Marc . . .'

'I thought I was doing the right thing,' he said awkwardly.

Martin ran to his room. Christmas was over. Jeanne went to comfort him; he wasn't upset, just shocked. From the other side of the door, Marc tried to apologise, but the damage had been done.

A little later, Jeanne joined Marc in their room.

'How could you do that?'

'I thought it was a good idea.'

'A good idea? Giving a *Harry Potter* book to my son was a good idea? You know what he's been through!'

'Exactly. I told myself this was the best thing to do.'

'The best thing to do?'

'Yes, he needs to exorcise it. He needs to stop skirting around the problem all the time. You know very well it's not possible, so he should face it,' he continued, although he didn't sound convinced himself.

Even if his theory was intellectually sound, Jeanne felt that his methods were devoid of all sensitivity. Anxiously, she asked Marc to go and speak to Martin. Hugo grumbled from the corner. 'Oh, come on . . . it's just a book! He's such a pain, ruining Christmas over that!' This was what hurt Martin the most – that nobody understood. They thought his despair was just a tantrum. That was why he suffered in silence most of the time, without burdening anyone else with his personal tragedy. After a while, everyone calmed down. They chalked it up to a faux pas – it happens.

15

Jeanne was pleased with the turn her professional life was taking. The French were avidly following the American election, and she was asked to return to Washington. In Europe, nobody thought Bush Jr would be re-elected. For many, he had been the worst-ever American president; in terms of mediocrity, he was unparalleled.

'Darling, don't worry. I can take care of Martin just fine.'

'Are you sure? It's not a nuisance?'

'Of course not.'

'But when Hugo isn't here . . . I don't want to impose . . .'

'It will all be fine. And honestly, Martin is very independent.'

Marc had not only reassured Jeanne, but also assuaged her guilt. He had been so understanding that he had relieved her of the mental burden that had grown larger since John's death. She could leave with peace of mind.

During her trip, she developed the habit of taking a mid-afternoon break to call home to France. She needed to hear her son's voice, even if he didn't talk much – the smallest anecdote from school had to be dragged out of him. Then she chatted to Marc, who was decidedly more talkative. Unlike Martin, she often had to cut him off when he was in full flow on this or that subject. He was sometimes offended by her suddenly interrupting one of his stories, forgetting that Jeanne was in the middle of her working day. But strangely, these conversations bonded the couple; distance can make people feel closer. Compared to Jeanne's relationship with John, who didn't like to reveal his innermost thoughts, this was a marked change. She compared the two men of her life – it was only natural. She was sure that at a crossroads, one man would have gone left, and the other right. Marc made her feel protected, as though their relationship had the power to ward off disaster. But she had lost the thrilling uncertainty of her time with John. What she had now was certainly preferable in terms of building a new life, its foundations free of the poetry of doubts. Because yes – she did picture herself having another child. She could easily put her career on hold for a few months. But then she felt unsure again. She was in love with a new man who fulfilled her – why wish for more? It was a classic conundrum to ponder. Especially as Jeanne was witnessing such exciting events so far from her own continent. And that is perhaps why she began to lose sight of things.

Because she wasn't seeing the whole picture. In her defence, there hadn't been any warning signs. It all happened suddenly. Their first evening alone together, while Martin was watching television in the living room, Marc approached him. For a moment, he stood staring at the boy, saying nothing, lining up his shot. In the end he said, in a calm, low voice that was barely audible:

'I'd like you to go to your room.'

'What?'

'I'd like you to go to your room.'

'To my room?'

'Yes.'

'When?'

'Now. I'd like you to go to your room.'

'But . . . I'm watching something.'

'So turn it off.'

'. . .'

'I have some work calls to make, and I need quiet.'

Martin was surprised at his stepfather's cold, authoritarian tone. If he had said it differently, Martin could have understood the request. But something wasn't right. Even the politeness of his sentence, the slow, careful way it had been hammered home, highlighted the feeling that it was a threat. Furthermore, he had trouble understanding the remark. Marc could have made a quiet phone call in his room. Why did he need the living room? It was as though Marc wanted to confine Martin to his bedroom. The boy felt it best to avoid further discussion.

He turned off the television and complied. Lying on his bed, he tried to understand. Perhaps Marc had had a difficult day, or had received some bad news. Children can quickly become outlets for their parents' frustration. But something about the series of events was still incomprehensible. Martin heard no sound in the apartment; nothing that suggested phone calls in progress. Not knowing what to think, eventually he fell asleep.

16

For some other unimportant reason, Marc repeated his demand the following evening. As soon as dinner was finished, he sent Martin to his room. This time, he added:

'And not a word to your mother, okay? Okay?'

'. . .'

'I'm talking to you.'

'Yeah, I heard you.'

'Don't you dare repeat this to your mother. This is between us.'

Martin was motionless for a moment, in shock. Before him was a completely different man from the one he thought he knew. Yet dinner had passed without incident. They had each talked about their day – a superficial discussion, certainly, but not one that gave any hint of the U-turn that followed. Marc had suddenly changed his attitude. Erratic behaviour was much more frightening than consistent aggression. From that moment on, Martin would never be able to predict which man he would find before him – a sort of Russian roulette of moods. Once he was in his room, he tried to downplay the situation – but was that even possible? Marc had clearly told him not to say anything to his mother. This betrayed the fact that Marc knew there was something illicit, something objectionable about his behaviour. Perhaps this was his idea of parenting . . . No, Martin had seen how he acted around his own son, and it was quite the opposite. You could even say he lacked authority over Hugo, letting him get away with everything. So what then? What was going on? Perhaps Martin should have been outraged, should have rebelled: 'No, I don't see why I should go to my room.' He could also have threatened to tell his mother. But he said nothing. Out of fear, most likely, but also for another reason: he felt that his mother was happy. He didn't want to ruin that. It was becoming an unsustainable equation: would his misery be the price he had to pay for his mother's happiness?

The next evening it was worse. Marc sent Martin straight to his room to eat dinner; he didn't want to see or hear him. For the moment, the abuse consisted of a geographical confinement. He was marking out the territory, the way that hunters do. Before falling asleep, Martin thought again about Christmas. It was clear now that Marc's present had been an insult, disguised as an innocent blunder. But why? What was its purpose? To push him to the edge, to get rid of him, to send him to boarding school? He couldn't understand it. As so often happens in such cases, rather than question his aggressor's mental stability, he started to doubt his own. Had he done something wrong? He must have. There was no other explanation. An illogical guilt took hold of him. Perhaps he and his Harry Potter phobia were insufferable. He thought he hadn't involved anyone else in it, but he must have been wrong. It must all be his fault.

17

When Jeanne returned, the play-acting of normal life resumed. The blended family ate dinner together, and the atmosphere was a happy one. Marc occasionally gave Martin a menacing look, whereupon Martin would lower his head. All he wanted was to shut himself away in his room. The consequences didn't take long to show. His school marks plummeted; he lost weight. Worried, his mother wanted to take him once more to a psychiatrist, but he refused, saying that it hadn't worked out the first time. Martin hoped that things would sort themselves out, but in the spring, Jeanne announced another week-long reporting trip. Given how fragile her son seemed, she was reluctant to leave, but eventually she set aside her worries. She couldn't not go. If she didn't take this chance, someone else would beat her to it. The newspaper wasn't lacking in ambitious reporters. So, to make herself feel better, or perhaps to relieve her conscience, she rationalised: Martin's recent attitude must just be an adolescent crisis; everyone went through them. Difficulties at that age were nothing out of the ordinary.

This assessment was further reaffirmed by Marc's reassuring words.

'It's normal. Teenagers always withdraw a bit at around fourteen, fifteen years old.'

'Not always. Look at your son, he's the life and soul.'

'Hugo is certainly less tortured. But he's also much less mature. Martin has grown up very fast because of everything he's been through. You might see the negative side, but I think he's very sensitive, and very clever.'

'You think so?'

'Yes. We talk a lot when you aren't here. He's very resourceful, I'm telling you.'

'Oh yeah? He talks to you?'

'Of course.'

'And what do you talk about?'

'We have our secrets . . .' he said with a smile, which gave Jeanne hers back too.

That evening, she went into her son's room. As she walked towards his bed, she had a fleeting memory of Martin as a baby. Everything still seemed so fresh in her mind; she saw herself rocking him, telling him stories, soothing him when he was sad. When she was sitting next to him, she said quietly, 'I'll only be gone for a week, my darling. It will go by quickly.' She kissed him on the forehead, and then turned off the light.

18

The days would become interminable. This time, Hugo was there too. Martin found he had changed since the previous week. He had gained some weight and seemed rather pink, with his hair falling into his eyes. He reminded Martin of someone . . . but who? Suddenly, an image came to him. It was Dudley, Harry Potter's tyrannical, rude cousin. The character that Harry had described in the first book as a 'pig in a wig'. There was clearly a strange similarity between them.

This could have simply been a passing thought, but it was one of a series of unnerving events. Since his failure at the audition, Martin's life had been plagued by worry and solitude, much like Harry's before he went to Hogwarts. And he had already been accosted by people telling him he looked like Daniel Radcliffe. Lastly, he remained traumatised by the loss of his father, by the fact he had become an orphan of sorts. True, he hadn't lost both of his parents, but the emotional cut was just as deep. And now he was being mistreated, just like Harry when he lived under the tyranny of his aunt and uncle.

That same evening, Martin found the words to describe how he was feeling.

'I'm turning into Harry Potter.'

Is it possible to become a real-life embodiment of a fictional character? Martin was starting to believe so. He had come so close to winning the role because he had all the qualities to personify Harry. And now he finally was – but in real life. He began to wonder: 'Should I read the other books in the series to find out what's going to happen to me?' The beginning of the book tallied perfectly. Vernon and Petunia Dursley left their nephew Harry to rot under the stairs, even though there was a spare bedroom in the house. But their son, Dudley, needed two: one to sleep in, and one to store his toys in. Martin, too, had been confined – not to a cupboard, of course, but to a restricted area of the apartment. And this was only the beginning, he realised. The stranglehold was only going to get tighter.

Just like Dudley did to Harry, Hugo began to bully Martin. With Jeanne gone, he had free rein. In truth, he too was being manipulated by his father. Marc told his son: 'Come on, let's go and tease him a bit. He needs to learn to laugh at himself!' They began to leave J. K. Rowling books lying around the apartment and spent dinners discussing the happenings at Hogwarts. Martin would then leave the table, taking refuge in his bedroom as he heard them saying: 'Ooh, he's so touchy!' He stuck his head under his pillow to try and muffle the sound of their treacherous words. He wished he were stronger, wished he could appear indifferent in the face of the two laughing monsters, but he couldn't. Every mention of Harry Potter felt like an assault. It was easy for them; he was a victim with such an obvious weakness. He offered up his suffering on a plate.

Martin borrowed a book about bullying from the school library. He recognised his own experience as he read the testimonies of the victims who, like him, felt responsible for it. He had to stop thinking everything was his fault. The most important thing now was to find the courage to tell his mother. Yes, that was what he must do, without fear of reprisals. He would tell her everything, and she would take immediate action. Furious, she would tell this madman to leave. It would all be over, and their life would resume as before. Martin imagined this confession over and over – what a relief it would be. He already knew every sentence of it, every comma, every breath. But when his mother returned from her trip, he became incapable of speaking. It wasn't so much that he didn't want to ruin her happiness, but rather because of something like shame. Yes – he felt so ashamed that he couldn't speak. In any case, Jeanne's return marked the end of the harassment. As soon as she came back, his hell vanished. They re-established their phoney paradise.

19

The month of May saw the start of the intensive marketing campaign for the release of the third film in the series, *Harry Potter and the Prisoner of Azkaban*. This time, it was no longer Chris Columbus at the helm, but Alfonso Cuarón. J. K. Rowling herself had suggested his name to the producers, having enjoyed his film *Y tu mamá también*, and his work with teenage actors in *A Little Princess*. Incidentally, she would mention in an interview years later that this film remained her favourite. Excitement had been growing steadily since the first images of the film were revealed. The films were entering the darker side of the story, a side which would only intensify. Martin saw in this an echo of his own personal tragedy. Dementors, powerful destroyers of beauty and happy memories, were circling around him. There was something of Voldemort in Marc. J. K. Rowling wove in her own suffering through these forces of evil – the way she had felt during her mother's slow decline. Martin identified with this, too; cancer, the embodiment of evil, had defeated his father.

Truth and fiction were muddled together in his mind. He was out of his depth, and the constant reminders of Harry Potter were making it hard for him to keep his head above water. This time, it seemed even more difficult than usual. No one could be unaware of the film's imminent release on 2 June 2004. The first two instalments had each sold close to ten million tickets in France. It was likely this would happen again – this number represented one in seven French people – and surely every teenager in the country would go to see it. For Martin, it was too painful a period to live through. It was still impossible for him not to imagine himself in Daniel Radcliffe's shoes. He begged his mother to let him stay home from school for a fortnight.

At first, she tried to reason with him; it was excessive, and besides, it was inconceivable. It already upset her to see him with no friends; staying at home was clearly another level. But he had never been capricious. This request was born of necessity. Distraught, she finally decided to give in to her son's pleas. Of course, she couldn't give an honest explanation to the headmaster. She couldn't imagine saying, 'Martin can't come to school at the moment, because a new *Harry Potter* film is coming out.' So she claimed he was in poor health and needed rest.

So Martin spent two weeks alone at home. His only fear was that Marc would take time off and stay with him all day, but thankfully this didn't happen. His mother called him regularly, and he reassured her. His decision to hide away from the intensive marketing campaign had been the right one. While Jeanne had initially thought Martin's request ridiculous, she now understood him. Not only did she see posters all over Paris, but she also saw how many products there were promoting the series. For example: she bought a tube of Colgate toothpaste without realising the brand was partnering with the film. Luckily, she noticed this at the last minute and was able to throw it away before her son used it. Even brushing his teeth had become difficult. As for Martin, he was avoiding all media – no radio, no newspapers and definitely no television. He wasn't wrong to do this. The actors were making constant appearances, talking about their hectic lives. Telling the story of their magical adventure was just as much a part of it as praising the virtues of the film – it all added to its mythical quality. Daniel Radcliffe even declared that the set of the film was 'the greatest playground in the world'. If every child on the planet dreamed of being in his place, what about the one who so nearly was?

20

Unfortunately, Martin's efforts to avoid the news were constantly being sabotaged. When Hugo got home from school, he went straight to Martin's room to tell him this or that anecdote; for example, that he had seen a news report about the hysteria provoked by the film's trailer in South Korea.

'It's nuts! It's like they're rock stars!'

'. . .'

'People screaming their names, girls are fainting. It's crazy what's happening to them!'

'. . .'

'You must be really sick of hearing about it . . .'

Martin pushed him away, wishing he could block access to his bedroom so he didn't have to put up with these malicious intrusions, but it was impossible. Marc had taken away the key, thinking that children shouldn't lock themselves away. So anyone could enter his territory whenever they felt like it. Their harassment no longer had any boundaries.

On the Thursday evening of the second week, Jeanne phoned to say she had been delayed at work. Martin immediately had an intuition that he would pay dearly for this hold-up, and he was right. Marc came into his room.

'You could have laid the table at least. Since you've done bugger all today.'

'. . .'

'He's a very convenient scapegoat, your Harry Potter. I've never heard such a lame excuse.'

Martin went to the kitchen and laid the table. That evening, Hugo and Marc decided to quite simply rename him Harry. All through dinner, they alternated between 'Harry, can you pass the salt?' and questions such as 'All right, Harry? Did you have a good day at Hogwarts?' They sniggered idiotically, proud of their pathetic digs. Martin still couldn't understand their logic; he was visibly shaken, almost dazed. He wished he could adopt Harry Potter's impassive attitude when confronted with his aunt and uncle's verbal abuse. He had just got up to return to his room when Marc stopped him coldly, saying, 'Stay at the table! We haven't finished!' His tone had suddenly changed

— there wasn't the slightest trace of supposed humour. Even Hugo didn't seem to really grasp what was happening. Martin stared at his plate, not moving. The silence lingered for a moment, but there was still a final blow to come, to finish the job. Marc sighed: 'You don't move, you don't speak, it's crazy. You're acting exactly like your father.'

The torturer knew perfectly well that he had gone too far. He had touched Martin's most sensitive nerve. After the moment he needed to take in what had just happened, Martin began to shout, over and over again: 'That's enough! That's enough! That's enough!' Then he pushed Hugo, who fell off his chair and hit his head on the floor. It seemed that nothing could stop Martin's rage. Marc stood up too — not to help his son up, but to slap Martin — a sharp, violent slap. Martin looked daggers at him and left the kitchen. Hugo stood up without saying a word, and was comforted by his father. 'That boy is completely hysterical!' Marc said, although he sounded unsure. He knew that Jeanne would be home soon, and that the matter wasn't likely to end there.

Martin examined his reddened cheek in the bathroom mirror. The mark was clearly visible. He would tell his mother everything. Yes, this would be the end of his silence. Could Marc read his mind? He came to him now with a demeanour that seemed completely changed. He took a flannel and held it under the tap before giving it to Martin.

'Here, put this on your face. It's cold water.'

'No.'

'What do you mean, no?'

'I don't want to.'

'Why not? It'll do you good.'

'I want to keep the mark. I want my mum to see it.'

'I wouldn't do that if I were you. Take the flannel like I said.'

'. . .'

'If you don't, I'll have to make you . . .'

For the first time, Martin felt real fear. He was pale, his heart beating wildly. Marc knew that it was getting out of hand. He couldn't help himself. He knew where this taste for violence came from, the perverse adrenaline rush he got from it, but he suddenly realised he was playing a dangerous game. He needed to rectify the situation, and fast.

'You know very well that I didn't want to hurt you. But you pushed Hugo. You started it.'

'And what you said about my dad?'

'You shouldn't have taken it that way. I swear, it wasn't meant to be negative. Your dad was an artist, a dreamer. Your mum has always told me that. I have a lot of admiration for him. I only meant that you were away with the fairies just then.'

'. . .'

'I'm sorry if you took it that way.'

'. . .'

'You know that I love you like my own son.'

'Then why do you keep calling me Harry?'

'It's a joke. In my family, we've always been like that. We tease each other, but it's all a bit of fun.'

'It's not funny.'

'Once again, I'm sorry if I hurt you. I promise we'll stop. Honestly, I just thought it would help you laugh it off. But I can see it didn't work.'

'. . .'

'Let's just forget about this evening, okay?'

All the while he was talking, Marc kept glancing at his watch. Jeanne would be home soon. He needed to calm the situation quickly. Martin was utterly confused. The words he was hearing sounded sincere, but he couldn't help being repulsed by this sudden tenderness. Marc added a few platitudes about the harmony of his and Jeanne's relationship, a happiness which shouldn't be disrupted by recounting this spoiled evening. So that was what he thought had happened: a spoiled evening. He had pushed him to the edge, humiliated him and insulted his father's memory all in the name of humour, of helping him 'laugh it off'. Marc hammered it home again. 'Think of your mum.' And at that precise moment, they heard the sound of the key in the lock. A few seconds later, Jeanne entered the bathroom, and upon seeing the mark on her son's cheek, immediately asked:

'What happened?'

'Nothing, my love. The boys had a fight. It happens,' Marc replied.

'Oh really? About what?'

'Oh, I don't know. I wasn't paying attention. I sent Hugo to his room.'

Martin said nothing. His mother came over to him. 'Are you okay, my darling?' Jeanne signalled to Marc to leave them. He exited the room, giving Martin a last threatening look. Once alone with his mother, Martin became mute, as though in a state of shock. She asked him over and over to tell her what had happened, but there was nothing to be done: he didn't want to talk. It took him a moment before he finally replied: 'It's nothing.'

21

Jeanne was worried. Her son was no longer going to school, and he was becoming increasingly withdrawn. Sometimes it seemed he had trouble expressing himself, and now he had fought with Hugo. She couldn't wait for summer to come, to take them out of their daily routine. A little later that evening, while saying goodnight to Martin, she mentioned the two of them taking a trip to Greece. He thought this a good idea, but he could only muster a few words to show his enthusiasm. Jeanne noticed a box on top of Martin's chest of drawers, one she hadn't seen before. To keep him talking a little longer before she left him for the night, she asked:

'What's in there?'

'Tinfoil,' Martin replied.

'Really? Why?'

'It's the tinfoil that Dad used to wrap my sandwiches in, when I took the train to visit you.'

'You kept it?'

'Yeah.'

'But . . . that's . . .'

Truthfully, Jeanne was lost for words. She found the gesture so touching. Martin had never told her about this precious collection. It brought a tear to her eye. There was so much humanity in her son.

22

Things changed dramatically. Marc went back to being kind, and Hugo followed his lead. The boy had clearly been primed by his father: 'We need to stop. He doesn't find it funny.' Deep down, Hugo felt relieved. He was happy to be back in cahoots with Martin – his step-brother, after all – and he promised himself he would never mention the painful subject again. This respite didn't stop Martin from being on his guard; he still felt fear in his stomach whenever he was alone with Marc. It could all start again. Perhaps that is the greatest achievement of a tormentor: to provoke a kind of muted terror without having to do a thing.

Martin was willing to live with this sword of Damocles hanging over his head, for the sake of his mother's happiness. Subconsciously, he felt that it was sadness that had really killed his father. So he let Jeanne bask in utter contentment, unaware that all was not well. One of the sources of her happiness was that her son had returned to school. As promised, he had gone back to classes after his two-week absence. He even claimed to be happy to be reunited with some of his schoolfriends. He gave this positive version of events to please his mother, but life was still difficult. In just two weeks, *Harry Potter and the Prisoner of Azkaban* had sold more than four million tickets at the box office, a phenomenal amount. On the other hand, if Martin had feared it would be the most talked-about subject at school, he had been worried for nothing. The fever had worn off, and everyone was talking about their holiday plans instead. In fact, Martin had been quite touched by the welcome he'd received on his return; everyone had been so kind. Both his classmates and his teachers thought something terrible must have happened for him to have missed two weeks of school. They asked him the reason for his absence, but he remained evasive. Some students even found his silence fascinating. It was a lesson for those who wished to become popular: people always think the quiet ones have the best stories.

With all this attention on him, Martin almost felt like Harry when he first arrived at Hogwarts. Everyone wanted to get close to the famous wizard that Voldemort had failed to kill. And yet Martin remained alone. In truth, his destiny was unfolding in the opposite way to Daniel Radcliffe's. The actor must lead an intense life, made up of endless meetings, travelling and pleasure. His day-to-day existence had enough riches for two lives – reducing Martin's to zero. The casting had pushed the two boys into a devastating imbalance.

Martin was lost in these thoughts when, on the Métro on the way home from school, a man handed him a flyer.

WHATEVER YOUR PROBLEM, CONTACT HIM:

Professor Cissé M'Béré

VERY GIFTED VOODOO HEALER

A holy man of great power, handed down from his ancestors. His results are garanteed at over 100% or your money back. If a problem tries to evade him he will hunt it down ruthlessly. He has thirty year's of experience and will solve the problems that trouble you. His consultations are profound and precise. HE IS NO STRANGER TO PROBLEMS OF LOVE. Unreqited love or the return of a loved one who will ask your forgiveness for the rest of their life. Work problems can also be solved with a click of his fingers. Fatigue, bad boss or bad employee. All will dissapear. Hair loss, ill health, fertility problems. Every problem as a solutin. Exorcising of demonic sim cards, playstation microchips, parking fines, imigration problems . . .

100% SATISFACTION GARANTEED IN ALL AREAS!!

Evidently it was the holy man himself walking through the train carriages. He wore a stack of necklaces and a ring on every finger. A veritable Dumbledore of the Métro Line 12. Perhaps what this man said was true – perhaps he had the solution to Martin's problem. Strangely, Martin didn't think about fighting Marc. His mind went straight to Harry Potter. That was where his obsession lay; that was where he needed help to 'hunt it down ruthlessly'. But how? Should he stick pins in a voodoo doll of Daniel Radcliffe? Perhaps the actor would fall ill . . .? No, no, he didn't want to do him harm. So what then? There had to be a less extreme solution. The professor could cast a spell on him, so he could no longer act . . . Yes, that was it. Turn Daniel Radcliffe into a bad actor. It would be a disaster; Warner Bros. would start panicking. He would no longer have the right intonation, and all his movements would be wooden. They would have no choice but to ask Martin to replace him. For just a couple of stops, lost in a reverie of the supernatural world, Martin saw himself taking Daniel Radcliffe's place. As he came out of the Métro station, he crumpled up the paper and threw it in the bin.

23

Summer arrived. When they left for Greece on 5 July 2004, Martin and his mother found themselves once more in the midst of an outbreak of mass hysteria – but this time, it was nothing to do with Harry Potter. The Greek national football team had just won the Euros for the first time in history. What a strange feeling it was to go searching far and wide for calm and serenity, only to find yourself in the middle of an enormous nightclub. Thankfully, they took the ferry from Athens to the island of Santorini, with its black-sand beaches. Martin used the occasion to take up free-diving. Just like in Greenland the year before, he seemed irrevocably drawn to anything that would allow him to escape the world. Down in the depths, he felt a paradoxical sense of elevation. In the evenings they ate dinners of fish and aubergines on the terraces of small, charming restaurants. The picturesque setting was so perfect that you could even hear someone playing a bouzouki in the distance. Jeanne didn't look at the breathtaking scenery, but instead at her son's face, finally at peace. That was what she had come here to find.

In August, they joined Marc and Hugo in Provence. Martin was apprehensive about the reunion, but everything went fairly well. His stepfather took the opportunity to apologise once more, putting his lapse down to stress and a moment of madness. To finalise their reconciliation, he even gave Martin a mini portable DVD player, so he could continue watching films over the summer. Jeanne and Marc had rented a beautiful house in the Luberon. On arriving, they were astounded by the charm of the place, and its huge garden. They coped with the heat by dashing to the banks of the nearby river. The boys even built a sort of raft that allowed them to drift along in the cool water. During those times, the adults made love in their room beneath a makeshift mosquito net. The holiday passed in this way, in a painless, slow rhythm. In the evenings, they lay down on the lawn to look at the stars, each person lost in their own thoughts. Martin's summer had been a good tonic, and even though he still had a lot of pain, he thought for the first time that, someday, he might find happiness. He wanted to believe it. What's more, no new film had been announced for the near future, and *Harry Potter and the Half-Blood Prince* wasn't due to be released until July 2005. It gave him time to catch his breath.

24

At the end of August, a few days before the schools went back, Marc suggested one last barbecue, on their balcony at home this time. Jeanne thought it was a 'marvellous' idea. She was often overly enthusiastic in an attempt to encourage her son. But Hugo and Martin were delighted with the idea, which would prolong the holiday feeling for a while. Jeanne made a Greek salad, in homage to the start of their summer. The barbecue set-up was sophisticated, with a two-tiered grill – lamb cutlets on the bottom, potatoes on the top. The starry nights and the cicadas were lacking, but it promised to be very pleasant nonetheless.

'Come and eat, it's almost ready!' Marc shouted, as though raising his voice would automatically grant him the status of competent chef. The boys came running towards the balcony, while Jeanne put the condiments on a tray. That was when Marc said to Martin:

'Lucky you had that tinfoil in your room.'

'. . .'

'I completely forgot to buy any! And without yours, I wouldn't have been able to cook the potatoes.'

Marc knew, of course, the significance of that tinfoil. Two months earlier, just after the fight between the two boys, Jeanne had told him what she'd discovered. 'It's so sweet. Martin kept a souvenir from all the sandwiches his father made him.'

Marc feigned emotion at this, praising Martin's sensitivity. He couldn't have forgotten. And the way in which he announced his malicious act left no room for doubt. He had waited until Jeanne's back was turned. Watching his mementos burn, Martin was devastated. The vestiges of his father's love. He couldn't move, his pain was so great. The attack felt even more violent given that he had lowered his guard lately. And here the hatred was, suddenly re-emerging, grabbing him brutally by the throat. He wanted to say: 'But why? Why would you do that?' Was there any justification for this cruelty? After the book Marc had given him for Christmas, and the insult to his father's memory, now he was witnessing the vandalising of the thing he held most dear in the world. He watched the tinfoil burning as though it were his own body being consumed.

Suddenly, Martin seized a barbecue skewer and plunged it into Marc's arm. He screamed in pain. Jeanne came running towards him – blood was pouring from his gaping wound. Marc rushed to the bathroom to make a tourniquet to stop the bleeding, yelling all the while, 'He's completely nuts!' Hugo, in shock, followed his father.

After a moment of stunned silence, Jeanne gathered her wits. On her knees before her listless son, she cried: 'What have you done? What have you done?' She repeated this over and over again, as if the cumulative effect of the words would help it all make sense. But her son didn't reply; he seemed possessed. In the end she slapped him, like she had seen in films: an action that would bring someone back to reality. But it changed nothing. On the contrary, he threw himself to the ground and rolled around, as though gripped by madness.

Marc and his son took a taxi to the hospital. Because of what had happened, he hadn't thought to put out the barbecue, and a suffocating smell of burning now filled the room. Jeanne was at a complete loss. Her son wouldn't come to. He was muttering something incomprehensible. Seized by panic, finally she decided to call an ambulance. Surely an injection or a sedative would calm him down. Twenty minutes later, two paramedics entered the apartment. When he saw them, Martin's confusion intensified. Again he saw his father collapsing in the grocer's. When two paramedics arrived, it meant someone was going to die. The pain sent him into a stupor, without even providing the relief of unconsciousness. He was lucid, far too lucid to want to survive all this. When they approached him, he struggled. There was no other option: he had to be taken away.

Jeanne held her son's hand in the ambulance. She looked into his eyes but didn't recognise him in them. They headed to the psychiatric emergency wing. During the journey, they had given him an injection and Martin had dozed off. As it was the end of August, there was no traffic, and it only took a few minutes to arrive at Pitié-Salpêtrière Hospital. Martin was carried to reception on a stretcher, his mother walking robot-like at his side. Before they went through the door, he opened his eyes, just in time to read the sign:

HÔPITAL PSYCHIATRIQUE

His vision out of focus, he saw only the initial letters, which spelled:

H P

That's what he saw: HP.
Yet another sign.
HP, for him, could only mean:

HARRY POTTER

PART THREE

1

Given the seriousness of Martin's psychological state, the junior doctor found him a bed in the Simon unit, the department for child and adolescent psychiatry. Martin found himself with a dozen teenagers in a secure facility. He had injured Marc's arm, but he could just as easily have stabbed him in the stomach or the lung. Jeanne was in shock, and was also pained at not being able to see her son. Visitors were not allowed at first. After two days, she finally met Dr Namouzian, one of the doctors in charge. Jeanne could read her first name on the badge pinned to her white coat: Nathalie. Jeanne clung to this name, the first sign of humanity she had come across in this place in the last forty-eight hours.

The conversation between the two women went on for a long time, despite Jeanne's fatigue. She spoke of the trauma surrounding John's death, and the feeling of failure that hadn't left Martin since the painful audition. The psychiatrist listened compassionately to the distressed mother's tale. She was used to these situations. She wrote down 'Harry Potter' in her notebook. The name rang a bell, of course, but nothing more. She was more into Éric Rohmer than Harry Potter. So, it was possible to live your life oblivious of the phenomenon. Her first feeling was simple: the causes and conditions of a rejection were not important, but the rejection itself must not be minimised. She knew perfectly well that people could die from not feeling wanted, or valued, or chosen. Jeanne was overwhelmed with emotion – she felt listened to, and supported. But she still had nothing that could help her understand what her son had done.

Naturally, the psychiatrist asked: 'How is Martin's relationship with his stepfather?'

'Very good. We just had a wonderful holiday together.'

'Have there ever been signs of tension between the two of them?'

'No, never.'

'How has your partner taken this aggression towards him?'

'. . .'

Marc had returned from hospital two days earlier with his arm bandaged. The wound had caused significant blood loss, but it wasn't deep and there was no nerve damage. That was the one positive in the whole shebang. Jeanne again questioned Marc about the circumstances of the incident, but he seemed just as bewildered as she was.

'It's truly incomprehensible. He just came at me suddenly.'

'He must have had a reason. People don't just act like that.'

'Apparently they do.'

'And Hugo didn't say anything?'

'No, he was sitting quietly in the corner. I'm in shock too. It's like he suddenly became someone else.'

'. . .'

'You know, I didn't want to say anything before, but—'

'What?'

'I think this Harry Potter thing has turned him a little crazy.'

'Martin isn't crazy. Don't say that.'

'Yes, well, he refused to go to school when the film came out. Does that seem normal to you?'

'. . .'

'I'm just saying, his behaviour is getting increasingly erratic.'

'But you always told me you thought he was sensitive . . . That's a good thing, right?'

'Yes, of course. But I also think he lives in his own world. He can't always tell what reality is. I mean, look at my arm!'

'I know . . . I know . . .'

'It'll be all right. It just needs to heal.'

'. . .'

'I'll tell him I'm not angry with him.'

'Thank you. Thank you for being there,' Jeanne said softly, curling up against the man she loved.

Jeanne relayed this conversation, and Marc's point of view, to the doctor. Instinctively, Nathalie Namouzian felt that the woman sitting opposite her didn't have all the facts. In cases of blended families, she often encountered children who had been hastily declared unstable by their step-parent. Martin had no prior psychiatric history. His act of violence could be linked to a specific situation. Even though he had been admitted to the clinic in a worrying state, for the time being there was nothing to suggest any kind of psychological problem.

'When can I see my son?' Jeanne fretted.

'In a few days.'

'I wasn't aware that you could stop a mother—'

'It's protocol. We have to cut the patient off from their family environment.'

'But he needs me.'

'I don't doubt that for a minute. To be honest, you have all the rights when it comes to your son. You can even sign a discharge order and leave with him now. But on the basis of what I've seen, I strongly advise you not to.'

'. . .'

'As things stand, I think Martin could become a danger to himself.'

'You mean . . .'

'Just that he's safe here.'

'. . .'

Jeanne wanted to trust this woman. She had faith in her professional opinion. But it wasn't an easy decision to make. This situation had pushed her to the edge. At that moment, they heard a moan emanating from the corridor, and Jeanne thought: 'My son is in the nuthouse.' The doctor suggested she take all the time she needed to think about it, showing her to an empty office. The thought that Martin could be suicidal haunted Jeanne. Fifteen years earlier, she had given birth in London, and her life seemed destined for happiness. Now, John was no longer here, and her son was sleeping in a secure facility, dosed up with sedatives. She decided to leave him there and signed the paperwork consenting to his confinement.

2

Voldemort had murdered Harry Potter's parents, without managing to kill their child. He had simply marked him with an indelible lightning bolt on his forehead. This distinctive symbol surely implied a future meeting; the chance for a final battle.

Martin had attacked his tormentor, but it was he who had lost. Now he was alone in a room without the slightest contact with the outside world. The forces of evil continued to destroy his life. For much of his first night in the unit, reality and fiction continued to blur for him. Unused to medication, he was lost in the maze of his feverish mind. But the next morning, he was able to gather his thoughts. He felt no regret. Instead, he was filled with a feeling of liberation. Never had he experienced such anger. Everything would be different now. No matter the consequences, he would never live with that man again. And now he would have the strength to talk to his mother, to tell her about the harassment he had suffered. Armed with this new energy, he was sure he could put an end to his silence and fear.

This positive momentum felt like a new skin. He hoped for a day when he wouldn't be haunted by his failure. He had reason to believe that there was a solution somewhere. It would take him time, but he would find it – and it would be unexpected, to say the least.

3

Martin spent several days in the care unit without any visitors. He took walks in the garden, feeling protected in that environment. In the evenings, the sedatives knocked him out. But they were rapidly decreasing the dosage. From his first meeting with the psychiatrist, Martin had told her very clearly what he had done. Though he showed no regret whatsoever, he did admit his actions had been violent. His rapid return to reality had been accelerated by what he could see of the other young people there. Clearly, he didn't belong here. Some of them had attempted suicide; others had self-harmed. You could see how brutal their desire was not to go on living. But he found a great deal of comfort in their exchanges. Some conversations offered him a crack of hope. And the staff were kind. At night, two men with strong Polish accents were in charge of monitoring of the patients. No matter the hour, you could go and see them for a glass of water, or to discuss an existential question. They always tried to find an answer for these nocturnal uncertainties.

At last, Martin was reunited with his mother. Just as he had promised himself, he told her everything during their first walk through the garden. Several times she tried to interrupt him, asking, 'But why didn't you say anything before? Why?' But he wanted to get to the end of his long story first. He needed to express his innermost feelings, to free himself completely from what he had been holding in. Jeanne had to sit down on a bench, stunned by the confession. Even before the anger, her first feeling was guilt. How could she not have seen this? How could she have let her son suffer so? It was Martin who reassured her. They embraced each other, as though their bodies contained the words they couldn't say.

Martin returned to his room. As she left the facility, Jeanne felt as though she might faint. So she went into an office, the same one where she'd had to make that decision a few days before. History was repeating itself. She should go to Marc's workplace and hurl abuse at him, hit him, hold him to account. But she didn't want to hear his excuses. She felt disgusted at the thought of the words he would say. Paradoxically, her anger was far too powerful for a confrontation. She had to act right now – call the movers and flee immediately. Since she had returned to France, she had only ever lived in furnished apartments – she would be able to pack everything in less than an hour. Yes, that was what she must do. Flee, flee this instant. That night, Marc would return to an empty apartment. She would stay with a friend until she found a new home. Marc was bound to harass her with phone calls and messages, but she would not respond. Before going to sleep, she would take a long hot shower. She would wash herself, then wash herself again. That was the image in her mind at that moment, in the empty hospital office: her body underwater.

4

The following morning, Marc turned up at the offices of *Le Point*. Jeanne went down to reception and explained that if he ever dared come back, she would report him. Feigning ignorance, he tried to cajole her. As she turned away from him, he shouted: 'What did he tell you then? You at least owe me an explanation!' Faced with Jeanne's silence, he added: 'But how can you believe him? You know he's not well. He wants to break us up.'

She turned around at that, and glared at him: 'Don't you dare talk about my son again. Ever again.'

Marc was dumbstruck, then stammered: 'But I didn't know about the tinfoil! I mean, I forgot! You have to believe me, my darling . . .' As she moved towards the lift, he seized her violently by the arm. 'You have to believe me!' The security guard rushed over to restrain him, pushing him towards the exit. Just as he went through the security gate, he cried a pathetic 'I love you!' Jeanne was so very ashamed. She thanked the security guard, but lingered for a moment to watch Marc through the glass façade. He moved away, becoming first a dot, then a tiny dot. And then he was gone. She couldn't see him any more – at least, for the time being.

Once she was sitting in her office, she thought, thank God I didn't have a child with him. Every evening they had made love and she'd felt his body against hers, his treacherous body. For a long time afterwards, that thought would make her feel sick. One of her colleagues, who had got wind of the scene in the foyer, popped her head in to check everything was okay. Jeanne gave a faint, phoney smile, before locking her office door. She couldn't stand anyone else looking at her today.

5

Three days later, Martin left the hospital. Jeanne told him simply that he would never have to deal with Marc any more. She didn't recount the details of the scene in the foyer; she needed to banish it from the story of their lives from that point on. Within twenty-four hours, Jeanne had found a two-bedroom flat that had just become available, as the old lady who lived there was moving to a retirement home. So, they found themselves in surroundings that seemed stuck in the 1970s, eating dinner in the kitchen on a waxed tablecloth in improbable shades of brown and orange. From the living room, they could hear a clock loudly marking the time in a tyranny of seconds. In this escape from modernity, peace once again seemed possible.

They rediscovered the inseparable bond between them, each one protecting the other. Of course, at times it was difficult; it was impossible to come out of such a situation unscathed. Jeanne avoided mentioning that Marc continued to bombard her with messages which alternated between denial and confession. And Martin didn't tell his mother about his nightmares and nocturnal wakings. To get away from it all, they went to London for the weekend, tracing the footsteps of their past. At John's grave, their memories came flooding back in all their beauty and sweetness. They even had the chance to have a drink with Rose, whose hair was now orange. She told them that she was getting married soon – a perfect excuse for another trip to England. While Martin had often associated his babysitter with his trauma, now he remembered only the good times. Actually, he was thinking less about Harry Potter. In a sense, recent events had diverted his attention. He wondered, 'Will I have to endure worse pain still in order to stop focusing on the thing that makes me suffer?' As he floated this theory, he smiled slightly – a hint of British humour.

6

Towards the end of October, Jeanne was contacted by a British journalist who was planning to write a book about the genesis of *Harry Potter*. It would cover the period from the first words written by J. K. Rowling, up to the making of the film. The journalist's name was Peter Taylor, and he was studying the story of the casting process; he had researched the 'other kid' mentioned by Janet Hirshenson. Thanks to an information sheet on which Martin's parents' names were noted, the journalist had found Jeanne. 'My son doesn't want to talk about it,' she had immediately replied. He was insistent, and suggested he come and meet her in Paris.

Although she hesitated, for fear of reopening the wound, in the end Jeanne relayed this conversation to her son. Martin reiterated that he didn't want to share his story with anyone. But his mother suggested a new theory.

'Maybe it would do you good to talk about it.'

'. . .'

'And more than that – it would give you a place in this whole story.'

'A place? But I don't want people to think of me as the failure of the story.'

'You didn't fail. They just chose someone else.'

'It doesn't matter. I don't want to be quoted.'

'I'm sorry. It was just an idea.'

'I know, Maman. But it makes me sick to my stomach that I can't move on from this. I could tell you that I'm jealous, but it's much more than that.'

'What is it?'

'. . .'

'Tell me.'

'Sometimes I feel like my life has been stolen from me.'

Jeanne found this phrase horribly violent. She tried to get her son to admit that it was excessive. He had never before expressed his emotions this way, in such a blunt manner. How could you live with the idea that someone has taken your place? The feeling that you've taken a back seat? Eventually Martin toned down his words, but meeting the journalist was out of the question. So Jeanne asked Taylor to respect her son's wish for anonymity. In the book, he would appear as the 'other boy' or 'the boy who was almost Harry Potter'. He would remain between the lines.

7

Jeanne decided to stop trying to convince her son to talk. Instead, she respected his wishes, and avoided mentioning the blasted subject from that moment on. In general terms, she mastered the art of evasion. And it went without saying that she no longer used a broom to sweep the apartment.

The road to recovery would still be long. But Martin led a mostly normal school life, even if he had started the school year a month late. Committed to his desire to protect himself, he still avoided forming friendships. As he was never invited anywhere at the weekend, he spent most of his time watching films, so much so that he became quite a film buff. Sometimes,

Jeanne opened his bedroom door a crack and saw him sitting there in his bubble. Just like his father, nothing seemed to soothe him as much as this kind of conversation with himself. To lessen her son's solitude, Jeanne organised some dinner parties. Since she couldn't exactly tell the guests, 'Whatever you do, don't mention *Harry Potter*!' instead she invited dusty old political commentators, with whom they could converse about Myanmar or Ukraine in peace. In short, in trying to distract her son, she organised the most deathly boring evenings possible. That said, everyone was stunned at how well informed Martin was; he held forth with ease on the geopolitical issues of the time. Without knowing that he lived as though condemned by his past, they predicted a great future for him.

These predictions would prove correct. The following year, he passed his *baccalauréat* with distinction. And yet the weeks preceding the exam had been particularly stressful. He had got wind of philosophy topics linked to Harry Potter. In some schools, the exams had required the students to answer the question: 'Was J. K. Rowling a Sartrean?' This hypothesis was accompanied by an extract in which the Sorting Hat assigned each Hogwarts student their house. Was this element of chance within our choices an allusion to the philosopher's famous theory that 'existence precedes essence'? Having to answer such a question would have been disastrous for Martin. At any moment, even when he least expected it, he could be attacked by Harry Potter. He was relieved to discover his question was instead: 'To achieve self-awareness, do we need other people?'

The evening he received his results, they celebrated the good news with champagne. It was just the two of them, but they were happy with that. Until now, Martin had avoided questions about his future. He always told his mother not to worry, that he would find his path. Several weeks previously, he'd had to fill out a course choice sheet, and had signed up to the Faculty of Arts and History. But he knew, deep down, that he still intended to avoid interacting with people as much as possible. The last two years at school had been gruelling. So the question remained: what was he going to do with his life?

8

That summer, they returned to Greece – it had become their ritual. That August was particularly stifling, with temperatures regularly surpassing forty degrees. Worse still, the drought had caused over three thousand forest fires. It was unprecedented. All the European nations sent water bombers to support the Greek firefighters. From their hotel, perched on top of a hill on the outskirts of Athens, Martin and Jeanne watched the surrounding blazes. There was something frightening about being so spellbound by the drama.

They took the boat to Santorini once more. After a day spent scuba diving, Martin wondered if he should follow that career path. He could become an instructor like Kostas, who had taught him the skill, and spend hours like this, in the deep. What could be better for someone with a phobia of the modern world? Underwater, no one would come and speak to him about Harry Potter. But did he really want to devote his life to it? No. It would remain a hobby, a few hours' distraction in the summer, but definitely not a profession. So what else was there? Thinking of the François Truffaut film *Stolen Kisses*, he wondered if perhaps he could be a hotel night watchman. Living a nocturnal life would have an advantage: most people would be asleep. All through the holiday, he continued assessing jobs that would present a low risk of meeting people, but it wasn't until the flight home to France that it suddenly came to him.

9

As a creature wounded by a powerful worldwide phenomenon, Martin had found the ideal place to hide himself away. Ancient sculptures and classical paintings would be his new domain. The Louvre was the El Dorado of a world without Harry Potter.

He would become a museum attendant. He would be in a place steeped in the past, where no one would ever speak to him. He only had to email his CV to be invited to interview. Jacqueline Janin, who was in charge of recruitment, took on numerous students. She received Martin in her rather narrow office. She spoke quietly and was the type to apologise often. Having spent her entire career at the Louvre (some people had nicknamed her Belphegor), she was used to seeing all sorts of candidates come and go, but Martin's profile immediately struck her as atypical.

'I don't understand. With your *baccalauréat* results, why don't you want to continue your studies?'

'I feel like I belong here.'

'There's nothing stopping you doing both. Being a museum attendant isn't necessarily a stimulating job. And the Louvre is so busy – it's not easy.'

'. . .'

'We can always adjust your hours later on if you ever change your mind.'

'Thank you.'

'In any case, if you'll allow me to give you some advice – say that you're writing a novel.'

'Excuse me?'

'People are always curious. They'll want to ask you questions because you don't obviously fit into any box. So tell them you're writing a novel – that always works. It's the perfect alibi for anything.'

They parted on this rather curious advice. Martin thought the woman had shown him a lot of kindness; he would later understand why. For the moment, he would become a civil servant of the chairs and corridors. New starters were usually stationed in a draughty corridor, or sometimes next to the toilets. Martin didn't mind spending his early days in the least exciting parts of the museum. The more the management noticed you, the sooner you advanced towards the *Mona Lisa*. His diligence soon drew attention, and he was moved to the Egyptian rooms. Of course, Martin was still placed in a corner, but by contorting himself, sitting on the edge of his chair, he was able to catch the tiniest glimpse of a mummy, or an amphora. His professionalism was praised once more, and he was moved from his chair to a more permanent position next to a textile taken directly from the tomb of Tutankhamun.

One day, during his break, he went for a walk to see the *Mona Lisa*. As expected, people were buzzing excitedly around the most famous painting in the world. As he watched this spectacle, Martin thought: 'The *Mona Lisa* is the *Harry Potter* of paintings.' Outside this tiny frame, nothing else existed. His gaze swept over the other paintings in the Salle des États. To the attendant visitors, they were invisible. Martin identified with them; he too had been close to his dream before being plunged into anonymity. His fate was that of a painting hung next to the *Mona Lisa*. He approached one of them: *Portrait of Thomas Stahel*, by Paris Bordone (1500–1571), a sixteenth-century oil on canvas. The painter was unknown to him, and Martin couldn't find any information on Stahel when he looked him up later. Moved by this painting that nobody looked at, he felt an emotional connection with this Thomas Stahel.

While the Louvre was a refuge, it nonetheless had its difficult moments. One day Martin spotted, from a distance, a teenager in a Harry Potter T-shirt. Merchandising was truly a plague. Above and beyond the ubiquitous wizard costumes, Martin feared, for example, that the McDonald's on his way to work would suddenly start offering a Quidditch menu, or that the Zara in his neighbourhood would launch a collection in Hogwarts colours. At any moment, J. K. Rowling could reappear.

10

Jeanne was sorry that her son wasn't continuing his studies, but it was his choice. He was an adult now, and there was nothing stopping him changing his mind later on. In any case, it was a new stage in their lives. Now that Martin was going to work, his mother thought, 'It's time to leave.' Jeanne sometimes felt that she was overprotective of her child, and that her attitude had perhaps encouraged him to keep wallowing in his neuroses. But what could she have done differently? She had simply tried to help him to live his life, in spite of his social difficulties. It had to be said that the results weren't convincing. He relied on her, and everyday life remained complicated. So yes, leaving him was an option. Martin would be forced to live independently, and perhaps in doing so, would free himself of his fears.

For several months, *Le Point* had been asking Jeanne to become their Washington correspondent. The political situation in the USA was exciting. A completely unexpected voice had just emerged. A charismatic outsider had announced his candidacy for Democratic nominee on 10 February and was steadily closing the gap between himself and Hillary Clinton. For many, he had sparked a fever of immense hope. There was no doubt about it – she had to follow this man. She had to follow Barack Obama.

Things moved quickly. They gave notice on their apartment and Martin found an attic room. He had few possessions – some books, some films, some clothes – a material life quickly summed up. It was the same for Jeanne. She sent a few boxes ahead, across the Atlantic. Now her departure was imminent; at first, they had discussed the practical details of this upheaval lightly, as though the actual event would never happen. But sometimes we must believe in the reality of our words. The day Jeanne left, Martin accompanied her to the airport.

'You know that if you have a problem, you can call me and I'll come straight back,' said Jeanne, before going through customs.

'Yes, Maman, I know. You already told me.'

'Okay, okay.'

'Right, off you go. You'll miss your flight.'

'I'm going, my darling. I'm going to miss you so much.'

'I'll miss you too, Maman.'

'I'll call you when I land.'

'Okay.'

'Ah no, it will be night-time for you. I don't want to wake you up.'

'Okay, we'll speak later on then.'

'In that case I'll wait until it's your morning . . . but then it might be late for me . . .'

'Maman! You're really going to miss it!'

'Okay, I'm going.'

'I love you.'

'I love you too.'

They hugged for a long time. Then Jeanne went through customs. On the walk to her departure gate, she kept turning around. Again and again they waved goodbye to each other. Just before losing sight of Martin, Jeanne thought: he looks so much like his father.

11

At the other end of the room Martin was sitting in, one of his colleagues, who was around twenty years old, glanced at him from time to time. This young woman evidently had the same shifts as him. Martin was, to say the least, unaccustomed to social interactions, and turned his head away – a gesture that she found touching. She imagined him to be a very shy person, with an exciting inner life. Mathilde – that was her name – eventually approached him and asked him quite simply if he liked working there. It took him a few long, stunned moments to find a response to this trivial question. Not only did he no longer possess the user manual for a simple conversation, but there was something else: he thought she was lovely. So often, lost in his solitary world, he had dreamed of meeting a girl who would love him, who would understand him. It had started rather badly, given he dared not even look at her. But since she had asked him the question, he finally raised his head, with a significant effort. She was standing in front of him, so close it startled him.

From that moment on, she often came over to him, and little by little they got to know each other. Mathilde was from Brittany, and seemed very proud of her origins. She was a student at the Beaux-Arts and was working at the museum in order to finance living in Paris. One day, she mentioned how much she adored the sculptor Camille Claudel, and launched into a long, feverish monologue about her admiration for Isabelle Adjani, who had played Claudel in a film. Thus, their conversations began to take shape. When she learned that Martin was not pursuing his studies alongside his job as a museum attendant, Mathilde asked him why not. Not knowing what to say, he stammered: 'I'm writing a novel.' The effectiveness of this response was impressive indeed. She understood his choice completely, and the question was resolved. The only snag was that Mathilde wanted to know more about his project. So Martin was forced to try writing some sort of novel, to be able to talk about the novel that he was not, in fact, writing. One thing was certain, even more so than literature: every day he liked her more and more. How could he have shut himself away from such beauty? To protect himself, yes – but now, Martin thought he would rather suffer with this girl than continue to live a solitary, painless life.

Actually, meeting Mathilde had done Martin a lot of good. Feeling appreciated by her, he began to grow into the best version of himself. He was a well-educated, witty young man, with plenty of charm. During a walk one evening, they ended up kissing. Martin took the memory of this kiss back to his attic room – a room he felt was far too small for what he had just experienced. The next day, they decided to spend Saturday night together. They would most likely have sex. Martin was nervous, of course; it was his first time. And Mathilde had much more experience. She had dated Loïc, her neighbour in Crozon, for three years. But she had decided to end things when she moved to Paris. She told him she didn't believe in long-distance relationships – but the truth was that she couldn't spend her life with a boy who thought Botticelli was a brand of pasta.

So they met at Mathilde's studio, which looked as if it had

come straight out of an Ikea catalogue. In the dim lighting, with some jazz playing in the background, they drank a beer sitting on the edge of the wooden bed. Mathilde got up from time to time to have a cigarette out of the window, where the smoke hung motionless in the air for a moment. After a while, kissing became their best conversational option. Martin's heart began to beat frantically; he couldn't believe how happy he felt. But just as they lay down on the bed, he noticed a pile of books. How hadn't he spotted those before? They were blindingly obvious now.

And.

Yes.

He saw a copy of *Harry Potter*.

It couldn't be.

It was *The Chamber of Secrets*, a title that was particularly apposite at that moment. Martin tried to control the mounting anxiety taking hold of him, but he couldn't. This sudden intrusion, when he was experiencing such happiness, completely unsettled him. He recoiled.

'Are you okay?'

'Yeah . . . yeah . . .'

'You know, it happens. It's normal to be nervous. I'm nervous too,' Mathilde tried to reassure him.

But it was no use: his mind was wandering now. His failure had come back to taunt him, had hunted him down in one of his rare moments of happiness. He wanted to brush off the feeling, it was madness; nothing could be more normal than having a *Harry Potter* book in your home. But no, it haunted him. Mathilde was talking to him, but he could no longer hear her. David Heyman's words were ringing in his head again, telling him he hadn't been chosen. The image of his childhood humiliation blurred the present. Still, always. A deafening buzzing filled his head and his vision clouded. He felt hot, so hot. Mathilde tried to help him, but he mumbled that he had to go. 'What? You can't be serious . . .' she sighed. Martin couldn't even respond. He stood up and left the apartment.

12

Martin spent the whole of Sunday brooding. He couldn't believe he had been so unsettled by seeing the book. At the very worst time, everything had come back to haunt him in a treacherous production of events. It's just not possible, it's never going to leave me alone, he thought, over and over again. He felt ashamed at having acted the way he had. Mathilde tried several times to reach him, but in vain. She needed an explanation – naturally. He didn't answer, tormented by the name appearing on his phone screen. The next morning, Martin waited for her to arrive. As soon as he saw her, he went over and immediately apologised for his behaviour. He promised to explain it all to her that evening, if she would agree to have a drink with him. But she shook her head. Mathilde could have forgiven his distress on Saturday night, but certainly not his silence on Sunday. She couldn't accept that he had left her like that, in complete confusion. A few days later, she landed an internship with an art dealer on Rue de Verneuil. She left the Louvre, and they never saw each other again. Martin had ruined everything.

13

On the phone to his mother, Martin only mentioned the positive aspects of his life. Yes, I'm fine, yes, really, Maman, everything is going well. But the truth was quite different. The episode with Mathilde had been a shock. He never wanted to go through anything like that again. Clearly, the symbol of his failure appearing at such a crucial moment had shaken him to the core. But he realised he would never be able to lead a normal life if he was reduced to nothing by such a small thing. He had to look his enemy in the face. He would go to a bookshop and buy a copy of *Harry Potter*. He couldn't go on living in fear of being confronted by such and such a situation, or of going to such and such a place. He could no longer bear his self-imposed geographical limitations.

At around ten o'clock one Saturday morning, he went out. As he strolled, he stopped here and there, calmly feigning nonchalance. Finally, he spotted his target: the Galignani bookshop on Rue de Rivoli. He went inside, as though it were nothing. He could be proud of this first step. As he browsed the books on the new-releases table, he noticed that none of the names were familiar to him, so cut off from the modern world was he. On the next table, he spied a novel with the title *Extension of the Domain of Struggle*. He loved this title; it sounded like a slogan for his plan of action. He loitered for a moment before the pile, undecided. Should he wander through the bookshop in search of the children's section? Or just ask for help? He didn't know how to proceed. Eventually, a bookseller came over to him. 'Can I help you?' Martin thought, No, that's kind, but no one can help me, but in the end he asked for the location of the *Harry Potter* books. The bookseller showed him to the shelf immediately, a task she must have to perform all the time. She added, 'We have the English editions too!' Why had she said that? How could she have known he was bilingual? Martin also needed to work on his slight tendency towards paranoia. The bookseller had simply mentioned this detail out of habit.

Faced with the pile of books, he chose the latest volume in the series: *Harry Potter and the Deathly Hallows*. Perhaps here was a sign of the resurrection to come. His goal was not to read it but to buy it, hold it in his hand, have it at home. After the panic he had felt at Mathilde's apartment, he'd anticipated this enforced confrontation would be more difficult. But no, it went quite smoothly. He paid without issue and left the bookshop. Mission accomplished.

14

But his desensitisation could not stop there. On 15 July, *Harry Potter and the Half-Blood Prince*, the sixth film in the series, would appear on screens. He still had this step to overcome: the cinema. However, it was better to practise, rather than jumping right in at the deep end. Though Martin occasionally went to art-house cinemas, he hadn't set foot in a large complex for more than ten years. The UGC at Les Halles was close to where he lived. Inside, a huge banner extolled the virtues of the current big hit, *The Hangover*. Martin thought the poster looked amusing, so opted for that film. Once he was sitting down, he looked at the young, joyful audience around him, impatiently awaiting the start of the film. He felt his heart sink – not because of what he was accomplishing, but because he realised how much his youth was passing him by. The comparison with other people's lives was painful. Fortunately, the room was soon plunged into darkness. He had completely forgotten there would be trailers before the film, and spent fifteen minutes in a state of great apprehension. By some miracle, no image of Harry Potter appeared. Finally, the film began.

Martin's cinema trip, a simple scouting mission, went smoothly. But it also brought about an important revelation. In the first scene of the film, the main characters wake up in a hotel suite in Las Vegas. They seem to have no understanding of their surroundings – they see a rooster strutting around, a tiger in the bathroom, and a baby in the cupboard. What has happened? They have no memory whatsoever of what they did during their night of heavy drinking. Complete amnesia. Martin wondered if perhaps that was the solution to his problem. For years, he had tried to avoid anything linked to Harry Potter. But couldn't he do what they did in the film? Go out, get drunk, remember nothing of the present. 'Drink to forget,' as the saying went. What if alcoholism was his way out? It wouldn't matter if a conversation upset him – he would have no memory of it.

It might seem strange to think like this – but Martin was simply searching for spaces where he could escape from himself. He loved the idea of living without remembering. They say ignorance is bliss. In any case, he had to try it. For years he had been looking for a way out. And nobody could help him, because his was a rare illness. He was the only human being who had almost been Harry Potter – the sole resident of that land. So he went home and put on a jacket, to give himself what he imagined was an evening look. But where should he go? After a quick look online, he chose a club in the Pigalle district, the Bus Palladium, and so he showed up there at 7:32 on a Saturday night. The bouncer explained that he was a little early. While he waited, he ordered a few beers in a nearby bar. Having little experience with alcohol, by the time he entered the nightclub he was stumbling. He headed straight for the dance floor, though it had been a long time since he'd danced. He swayed his body, trying to copy the other dancers. His way of moving was like a conversation that swung from a discussion of Nietzsche to a recipe for moussaka. A few people gave him amused looks, but he didn't notice. His plan was working marvellously; alcohol had taken away all his inhibitions. He even struck up a conversation with someone called Enzo, who had great artistic aspirations.

'I'm going to put on a historical show, about the Resistance! And it will be a cabaret, too . . . Yes, with dancing . . . and girls!'

'. . .'

'I'll call it Jean Moulin-Rouge!'

'. . .'

'What do you think? Huh? Huh?'

Martin would, of course, have no memory of this conversation. After a few hours, he began to feel nauseous. A waiter approached him and offered to call him a taxi. Martin found himself back in his bed with helicopter syndrome: the ceiling was spinning above his head. He rushed to the bathroom to vomit. His progress had ended with a pathetic bang. The next day was a Sunday of pure horror. What a strange idea for recovery it had been. What had come over him? Evidently, it was better to remain someone who suffered but stayed sober.

15

His recent endeavours had made little difference. Yes, he had been able to buy a book – but it was a tiny step on the road to the recovery he hoped for. For the time being, he had to go on living as he had before. Not a day passed when he didn't think about Daniel Radcliffe, at one point or another. His failure continued to get the better of him.

Several months went by in this way. Martin applied himself more and more to his job at the museum, working overtime whenever it was offered to him. Which was how something miraculous happened. Jacqueline Janin was on the verge of retirement. Since the interview, she had sometimes summoned Martin to her office to hear his news, but their relationship had remained superficial. No one at the museum knew that Jacqueline had lost her only son in a car accident fifteen years earlier; she had been a shadow of her former self since then. Had she seen in Martin – the dreamy, serious young man that he was – a reflection of her own son? Whatever the case, to her mind there was no doubt about it: he was the ideal candidate to take over her post. All that remained now was to convince the director, who was, needless to say, taken aback by her choice.

'Listen, Martin Hill is twenty years old. I want to trust you, but I think it's too early for him to take on this role.'

'I haven't asked for a thing in thirty years, as you well know. Believe me, he was made for this profession. He is a brilliant young man.'

'I don't doubt it. I can see from his CV that he received a distinction in his *baccalauréat*. In fact – do you know why he didn't continue his studies?'

'I think he's writing a novel . . .'

'Ah, okay. But that doesn't change anything. He doesn't have the experience.'

'Monsieur Loyrette, I understand perfectly. It is your decision, of course. But there is nothing stopping you from trying him out. If it doesn't work out, you can choose someone else.'

'. . .'

'I'm asking you as a favour.'

'Well, well . . . All right, we'll give it a go.'

'Thank you. You won't regret it.'

And that was what actually happened. Jacqueline Janin fought for Martin. Without applying, without even being interviewed, he found himself propelled towards a management position. He was offered the role, and very quickly the director realised what a good decision it was. Martin was praised for his incredible ability to choose the right people and lead them. Martin Hill knew better than anyone how to spot hidden talents.

Martin wanted to thank Jacqueline by taking her out to lunch, but she had left immediately to go and live in the South of France. From then on they would exchange a few friendly messages, to wish each other happy birthday or happy New Year, but nothing more. She had been a benevolent presence in his life, a sort of passing guardian angel. And it had done him the world of good to feel someone watching over him. Before leaving the museum, she had even said: 'Don't forget that I believe in you.' These words had moved him, like a promise of strength. Martin had long thought that he had suffered because of the Other's victory, but it was his own defeat that haunted him. He had spent a decade underestimating himself, imagining his life was a failure because *he* was a failure. Jacqueline Janin's incredible generosity had encouraged him to have confidence in himself. Of course, he had received plenty of love from his parents. But this was someone on the outside – someone, as it were, who had no emotional obligation towards him.

16

What if love was the answer? Feeling wanted, valued, loved – perhaps that was the antidote to his obsession with his failure. But, for that, he would have to meet a woman who could mend his heart. He set out in search of her. Naturally, he tried to reconnect with Mathilde, but she no longer wanted to hear what he had to say. So he kept an eye on the visitors to the museum, signed up to dating sites, and began taking slow walks in the street. But it was no use – there was not the slightest chance of meeting someone. Martin had simply forgotten one thing: it is well known that in order to find love, you have to stop looking for it. He came across an advert for a fortune-teller and decided to consult her. The woman inhaled deeply, as if she had to hold her breath in order to see the future right inside herself, and said: 'You will meet her in a kitchen . . .' Martin wanted to know more, but that was the only thing she saw. The information, pithy and mysterious as it was, had nonetheless cost him a hundred euros.

17

Like a casting director for the Louvre, Martin's new job consisted in choosing the museum attendants – an ironic post for someone who had suffered so badly from rejection. Certainly the stakes were lower; it was a far cry from the leading role in an internationally renowned film. Many of the candidates, especially the students, were just looking for a side job to earn a bit of money. But Martin was soon struck by something he hadn't expected – he wasn't the only person who had come to the museum in search of refuge. Just like him, men and women arrived there in the hope of fleeing the painful setting of the modern world. He found himself faced with a veritable army of second bests.

Among the applicants, he met a writer who had been a finalist for the Prix Goncourt in 1978. Patrick Modiano had won that year at the age of thirty-three, for his sixth novel, *Missing Person*. Since then, Modiano had enjoyed success after success, and captivated audiences during his television appearances with Bernard Pivot. For the loser, the Other's fame had meant constant awareness of his failure.[4] Exhausted by seeing the man who had fleetingly been his rival everywhere, in the end he had given up writing. Which was why he now wanted to hide away in a museum. This man's trajectory, so close to his own, moved Martin. He hired him on the spot.

All the losers of competitions that had attracted a lot of media attention had lived through the same suffering: a failure exacerbated by the omnipresent images of the winner's happiness. Yes, you could tell them: 'It's fantastic to have even made it to the final!' But no one could be happy with almost achieving their goal. It was better to stay in the shadows than come so close to the light. The bitterness was multiplied tenfold. The rejected parties returned to the depths of general disinterest, while the winner was dazzled by the attention of the world. Though a Goncourt was no match for Harry Potter in terms of scale, the hardships were nonetheless comparable.

A few weeks later, he recruited a former Miss France runner-up. In 1987 she had lost to Nathalie Marquay, who went on to become the wife of a famous TV news presenter. Normally, the winner would only be in the limelight for a year,

---

4   And he hadn't yet lived through what would be the ultimate torture: Modiano would win the Nobel Prize in Literature in 2014.

and the loser's suffering would abate at the end of this period of media frenzy – but in this case, it never stopped. Nathalie Marquay even competed in a reality TV show. Which is why, just like the unsuccessful writer, the runner-up of Miss France 1987 wanted to hide away among the paintings.

Martin couldn't believe it; he was recruiting his brothers and sisters in suffering. There was no bitterness in their conduct, only the desire to protect themselves from the onslaught of current affairs for a few hours a day. The candidate entering his office at that moment would be another example. Karim looked around the room nervously before sitting down. You could tell he was always on the alert. After looking through his CV, Martin asked:

'Are you an actor?'

'How did you know?'

'It's written here—'

'Oh dear, I must have sent you an old CV. I decided to give it up.'

'But you've been in a few films. Your career looked promising—'

'Yes, but that's all over now.'

'So you want to be a museum attendant?'

'Yes. I want to be in a place where . . . How can I say this? I don't know. People forget about everything here.'

'I understand. But it's not as easy as that. It's crowded, so you have to stay alert.'

'I can imagine . . .'

'Can I ask you a question?'

'It's what you've been doing from the start.'

'Yes, of course . . . but I wanted to ask you a more personal question.'

'Go ahead.'

'Who took your place?'

'What?' Karim asked, startled.

'Who took your place?'

'But . . . but . . . why would you ask me that?'

'The role – who got it?'

'But . . .'

'Which film was it for?'

'. . .'

'You can tell me.'

'I don't know why you would ask me . . . like that . . .' Karim stammered.

There was a pause, during which the young man didn't know what to think. For a fleeting moment, he wondered if there was a hidden camera. But no, that wasn't possible. He had come here of his own accord; nobody could have planned such a stunt. In a friendly tone, Martin repeated that he could tell him everything, that it would be strictly between them. Eventually, Karim confessed.

'*A Prophet*. It was *A Prophet* . . . the Jacques Audiard film.'

'And it was down to just two of you, I'm guessing?'

'Yes . . . but . . . how . . .'

'I know.'

'I don't really like talking about it, to be honest.'

'I understand.'

'. . .'

'Can we speak informally? We're almost the same age,' Martin said.

'Yes.'

'What was the other actor called?'

'Ta-har . . . I don't want to say his name.'

'Yes, I understand that too.'

'And he won two Césars. I'm so sick of it . . .'

Much later, Martin would tell his story to Karim, who wouldn't be able to believe it. To be rejected for Harry Potter seemed even worse than his own failure. He would suddenly feel as though he was sitting opposite patient zero of his own illness. But, for the moment, Martin continued to encourage Karim to talk. Just like Martin, the young actor had not gone looking for anything, to begin with. Jacques Audiard had seen one of his performances in another film and asked to see him. During their first meeting, they had just talked; the two of them had a connection, and Karim had left the encounter trying to control his excitement. Audiard's reputation was huge. He had already made several successful films, like *A Self-Made Hero* and *The Beat That My Heart Skipped*. Working with him was not only every actor's dream, but it could change the course of a career – perhaps of a life.

For Jacques Audiard, finding the actor for his new project was a real challenge. Evidently, he wanted a newcomer. A few weeks later, the director found himself with two actors left in the running. He was undecided, and conducted multiple auditions with both. Karim spoke of that time as both euphoric and nerve-racking. He had deeply researched the prison world, had worked on his gait, his vocabulary – he was absolutely ready to do anything to get the role. Audiard seemed impressed by the drive of the young actor, who for his part was starting to believe this could really happen. It was the chance of a lifetime. The role had been written for him, there was no doubt in his mind about that. And yet, in the end, Jacques Audiard had chosen Tahar Rahim. Who was he? No one had ever heard of him. This nobody had just stolen his dream. Karim fell into what he later recognised as depression. He stayed in bed for weeks, brooding on the wrong turn his future had taken. Those close to him tried to cheer him up; after all, it was still something that Audiard had noticed him, and would surely hire him for his next film. All the efforts and attention from the people around him were kind, but there was nothing they could say that would help him. He got back on his feet by himself and began to feel better. He resumed auditioning, motivated himself. But just like Martin, he suffered what might be called a second wave of failure, which would be even more powerful.

In May 2009, *A Prophet* was the hit of the Cannes Film Festival. The stunning revelation of the film's young lead actor was all anyone could talk about. A few months later, he won the double at the César awards: Best Actor and Most Promising Actor. It was huge. Rarely had a career been launched in this way, and with such unanimity. Every ounce of Tahar Rahim's success lowered Karim's spirits a little more. He felt motivated by rage and disgust. Even worse, his mother had left a gossip magazine lying around in their living room, showing the actor with a young woman, all smiles. The caption said: 'In addition to his success, Tahar Rahim has also found love on set with Leila. They never leave each other's side.' Karim stared at the photo for a long time, at the girl's face in particular. She was so beautiful that it just about finished him off.

Karim's monologue had lasted almost twenty minutes. Martin had tears in his eyes; he had felt every word in his very being. He stood up and put his arms around his comrade-in-despair. Then finally he stammered, 'It's okay, you're hired.' Karim backed away a few feet, as though he had suddenly come back to reality. He had never experienced such a bizarre interview.

18

Martin no longer felt alone, and that changed everything. He and Karim helped one another with their strategies for avoiding Daniel Radcliffe and Tahar Rahim, respectively. But it was still difficult. Now that the *Harry Potter* series was finished, the media endlessly scrutinised the tiniest facts about and movements of the main actor. There were hundreds of articles discussing the future of his career. 'What will he do now?' was the question the media world was obsessed with. So it would never end. Apparently he was working on a horror film, *The Woman in Black*. Martin was reduced to hoping that the actor's next films would be flops, so he would gradually be forgotten. He wished upon Radcliffe a career like that of Macaulay Culkin, who had had difficulty replicating the success of *Home Alone*. There were rumours that Daniel Radcliffe had succumbed to alcoholism, so there was still hope . . . which was quickly extinguished. The actor still gave regular interviews where he talked about the incredible adventure that was his life.

Martin could be proud of himself: he had survived seven novels and eight films. But the end of the series made no dent whatsoever in the hysteria – quite the opposite. There were endless petitions for J. K. Rowling to reprise her characters for another book. People speculated, people quibbled, people fantasised. There was every kind of commemoration and celebration. And to top it all off, a new series of films was announced: *Fantastic Beasts and Where to Find Them*, a *Harry Potter* spin-off. Martin was already sick of it.

19

A few months passed in this Janus-like existence of contrasts. Martin alternated between moments of fulfilment at work and moments when he doubted he would ever be able to lead a normal life. Until the day that Jeanne decided to surprise him. She missed her son too much; she couldn't stand only seeing him on a screen. She took a flight to Paris without telling him, went directly to the Louvre from the airport, took a photo of a painting and sent it to him. He might have wondered why she was sharing this painting with him, but he knew instinctively: She's here. He hurried out of his office, walked through countless galleries, weaving in and out of visitors, before finally finding himself by Titian's *Woman with a Mirror*. Yes, she was here. What she had done was so beautiful. Jeanne saw Martin then too, and they approached each other slowly. They embraced with such abandon that several Japanese tourists captured the moment for posterity.

20

But this wasn't just a visit. Jeanne had decided to move back to France – to be closer to her son, but also because she was tired of life in the United States. She hadn't managed to meet many people, whether friends or romantic partners – the country continued to elude her. In any case, the situation there had become less interesting. It was in the middle of Barack Obama's presidency, and his re-election seemed certain. On the other hand, in Washington she had met Dominique Strauss-Kahn a number of times, and was convinced that he would be the next president of France. So she had set about writing an essay about him: 'DSK, a French President Made in the USA'. A few months later, she would be forced to abandon her project.

They resumed their old habits, alternating between long walks and dinners at restaurants. Though Jeanne still skirted around the taboo subject, she'd had an idea that she wanted to share with her son. An idea based around the expression 'fighting fire with fire'. In truth, this thought hadn't come out of nowhere. Jeanne had recently discovered that a castle in Poland had been transformed into a Hogwarts replica, and that fans could arrange to stay there. In the same way that those afraid of flying could spend time in the cockpit to conquer their fear, it seemed clear to her: her son had to take part.

'Are you serious?'

'Yes, I am.'

'I don't see how this will make me feel better.'

'You told me that being able to buy a book or go to the cinema did you good. This would be the ultimate step. If you pass this test, I'm certain that it will be over for you.'

'This is bullshit.'

'My darling, it's been bullshit from the start.'

It had to be said: his mother wasn't wrong. His life was unlike any other. He was paralysed by the world's most famous book. Maybe Jeanne was right. A miracle could happen, and he could finally emerge from it happy. He didn't really believe it, but it was worth a try. If, in the worst-case scenario, he found it too hard, he could always turn back.

21

As he passed through small villages in Poland, Martin had the fleeting thought that he could settle here. CHANGE YOUR LIFE was the ultimate modern slogan. Never before had human existence been so fuelled by the need for constant change. Until now, people's fates had been, for the most part, linear; nowadays you saw electricians becoming yoga teachers and teachers opening cheese shops. In the little town of Je̦drzychowice, which seemed frozen in time, Martin could have a new future. Far from *Harry Potter*, he would find himself instead lost between Thomas Mann's *The Magic Mountain* and Isaac Bashevis Singer's *The Magician of Lublin*.

To keep his mind off things during the last few kilometres before Czocha, he went over the details of his itinerary again. The brochure indicated, among other things, that speaking English was obligatory in order to participate in the visit. Upon arrival, there would be a welcome drink during which participants would be told where their lodgings were – a Sorting Ceremony, just like in the book. Along with the accommodation, the package also included the loan of a wizard's robe. It was a basic model, and the wearer was at liberty to go in search of more sophisticated accessories. For that, you could go to Gringotts (the bank from *Harry Potter*) and exchange euros for golden Galleons, silver Sickles and bronze Knuts. Before the festivities began, there was time for a shopping spree in Diagon Alley. Beneath its playful veneer, this business was monetising every part of the fantasy.

Martin, who had come so close to the original set, prepared to enter the lair of its replica. The sour odour of the downgrade took hold of him. As he got off the bus, he was pointed in the direction of the castle, about a kilometre's walk away. While the majority of the visitors arrived by car, he shared the road with other pedestrians. He spotted a girl with red hair, a boy in a frayed frock coat, and another boy who was skipping along, seemingly talking to the insects by the roadside. In short, it all had the air of a procession towards an initiation to join a cult. The residents of the village stood outside their houses, watching them go past. It certainly made them laugh, seeing these stupid teenagers dressed up as amateur wizards. Martin would soon be reassured: those who had come on foot were the strangest. Most of the guests just came to have fun, to get close to the phenomenon that had shaped their childhoods.

22

Finally, he could make out the castle. On the long path that led to the main entrance, you could hear the legendary theme of the film, composed by John Williams. It was one of those tunes that has the power to enter your head and never leave again. On the front steps, a giant who must have been the Polish Hagrid welcomed each arrival with a big smile, handing them their welcome letter. The hall had been transformed into a canteen; although it was evidently smaller than the one at Hogwarts, the replica was still impressive. Everyone seemed spellbound; Martin was clearly in the realm of fans. A few were speaking strange words, while others were already attempting magic spells. Martin was one of the first to sit down. He had been expecting to feel much more unnerved, but in fact was handling the situation well. Eventually, he understood why. Usually he was always on the alert. Here, in the heart of it all, there was no sudden intrusion to be feared. The hostile environment was so unambiguous that it became normal.

After Polish Hagrid came Polish Dumbledore. His long white beard was clearly a cheap fake. As enthusiastic as they were, these part-time showmen didn't have Warner Bros.' budget. At the table, Martin was sitting with a young man who seemed shy, and a girl so chatty that she was evidently capable of talking to herself. She said everything she was thinking out loud, and eventually exclaimed: 'I hope we'll be in Gryffindor, it's the best house!' There was no irony in this statement: she seemed to be having the time of her life. This American, named Jessica, was an exact double of Hermione. Her wish was granted, testament to the power of positive thinking. A few minutes later, Polish Dumbledore looked in the Sorting Hat and announced: 'Martin Hill . . . Gryffindor!' Everyone applauded, though he didn't really understand what was going on. Jessica whispered: 'Great, we're together!' The duo was joined by the boy who was also at their table, a Czech redhead named Pavel. He too had been assigned to the same house. A sort of trio had formed, and Martin couldn't help seeing a similarity with the book. If his two sidekicks were Hermione and Ron, that meant that he was Harry.

After putting their things in the dormitory, Jessica said to Martin:

'You really look like Harry Potter. It's weird.'

'Oh yeah?'

'Don't act coy. I'm sure you've been told that before.'

'. . .'

'Don't you think so?' she asked Pavel.

'Yeah, you do,' he replied in a thick Czech accent, but Martin felt that he just didn't want to contradict Jessica.

Soon the whole dormitory was examining Martin's face, exclaiming, 'The resemblance is crazy!' So much so that one of the participants said:

'Oh, I get it! You're part of the experience!'

'Not at all,' Martin replied feebly.

'Yeah right!'

Martin was speechless, leaving the others excitedly discussing this far-fetched theory.

23

The following morning was dedicated to magical duels. Firstly, the participants had to memorise the spells – the majority already knew them. There were cries of 'Furnunculus!',[5] 'Riddikulus!',[6] and 'Levicorpus!'[7] Everyone waved their magic wands, but nothing happened. No tourist amid the Hogwarts decor was suddenly going to be able to make toads appear. At everyone's insistence, Martin was forced to join in. But he felt exhausted. He wasn't used to dormitories and had only slept for a few hours. And now they were expecting him to produce a miracle. The other guests clapped their hands to encourage him, chanting 'Harry! Harry!' increasingly overexcitedly. They had decided he was no longer Martin. Gradually becoming less clear-headed, Martin lifted his wand and searched for his target. He spotted a girl who was very tall and thin, as if drawn by Giacometti. He approached her slowly. Everyone held their breath. His target began to tremble; beads of sweat had already broken out at her temples. As a true fan, she believed she was face to face with the real Harry Potter. Maybe she was right? Martin felt possessed. In a kind of trance, he racked his brain, trying to remember a

---

5 Break out in boils!

6 Turn a Boggart into something ridiculous!

7 Dangle someone in mid-air by the ankle!

spell. Finally, he had a brainwave. He suddenly cried, 'Obscuro!'[8] staring at his victim. Immediately, the girl's large black headband slid down over her eyes, most likely due to the sweat. The effect was startling. The hubbub turned to silence – the music of astonishment. Something magical – supernatural, even – had just happened.

At lunch, at every table, that was all they talked about. The man in charge of the trip, the fake Dumbledore, approached Martin.

'It seems we have Harry Potter in our midst.'

' . . . '

'The resemblance is staggering,' he whispered, suddenly excited.

He himself was obsessed with the J. K. Rowling universe; he had created this place because he was such a fan. He tried to strike up a conversation, asking questions, but Martin evaded them with responses that were either short or inaudible. Every hour he spent here was stranger than the last. And yet, everyone was being so kind to him. He was discovering the feeling of being appreciated, of being popular, even. He should have been rejoicing, but he felt the opposite – the excitement he had stirred up in this bargain-basement Hogwarts just made him imagine how things could have been in real life. This trip was giving him the crumbs of a happiness that wasn't his own.

Jessica tapped him on the back: 'Hurry up, the Quidditch match is about to start!' A few minutes later, everyone was assembled in the castle's vast grounds. Polish Hagrid announced that the winner would take home the famous Quidditch Cup. Martin thought it rather bold that they had organised such an event; it wouldn't take the visitors long to realise that their broomsticks couldn't fly. Because Martin was Harry Potter, it

---

8   Place a black blindfold over someone's eyes!

was decreed that he must be good at this sport. Thus he was encouraged to be team captain, and was forced to accept. Jessica and Pavel were ecstatic, certain they would win with Martin as their star player. Martin looked at them for a moment, stunned by the strength of their conviction. They had to be crazy to believe in him so much.

The match began. It resembled a kind of dodgeball, with one major difference – everyone ran about with a broomstick between their thighs. Without really knowing why, Martin managed to move with disconcerting ease. He was better than anyone at placing himself behind an adversary to put them offside. Every time he scored a point, the hysteria around him grew. The chants of encouragement were incessant: 'Harry, Harry, Harry!' He ran in all directions, not knowing who he was, not even knowing the aim of this stupid game. He was lost in deepest Poland, sweating and dazed with fatigue, in a totally crazy situation. Having finally understood the rules of the game, it was up to him to score the winning point. That was when, to everyone's astonishment, he suddenly threw his broom to the ground. Why had he done it? In the middle of the deciding half, perhaps he was trying something new. A few people whispered that they had to trust him; there must be a strategy behind his action. After all, this was Harry Potter, in the flesh. Martin spun around, watching the crowd surrounding the field, avidly following his every movement. He let the freeze-frame of this image last a moment longer, and then suddenly gave a wild laugh. No one understood. How could he be laughing at such a critical moment in the match?

He left the pitch to looks of astonishment. By not scoring the last point, he had lost his team the match. 'Maybe it's another tactic,' a few irrepressible optimists wanted to believe. But no, they had to admit the truth: he was running away.

Two or three fans rushed to hold him back, but Martin threatened to curse anyone who stopped him from leaving. Afraid, the Potterheads backed away immediately. He walked alone to the dormitory, picked up his bag, and left the castle. On the return journey, he thought that this strange experience had had the benefit of confirming what he had always known: he should have been Harry Potter.

24

Martin recounted his adventure to his mother. Once again, to make her happy, he told her that it had done him good. In reality, it hadn't changed much. He could come close to J. K. Rowling's world, which was huge progress, but the bitter taste of failure lingered inexorably in his mouth. It seemed that nothing could free him from it. He would have to wait a little longer before finding the solution.

Martin also told Karim about his trip. Karim was amused, imagining the reaction of the participants around the sub-Quidditch field. He said:

'Maybe I could do that too?'

'Do what?'

'Fight fire with fire.'

'Oh, yeah.'

'But . . . for that I'd have to go to prison,' he went on, grinning.

They continued imagining strategies for forgetting about the Other, but light-heartedly. Together, they could laugh it off. It soothed Martin to feel understood. Deep down, Karim was much more than a friend; he was his prophet.

25

That evening, Karim invited Martin to come with him to a party. The hosts had put up a sign in the hallway of his building. Out of politeness, and to alleviate any annoyance to come, they had invited the neighbours to stop by for a drink. The kind of note you write without thinking that anyone would have the guts to gatecrash – but they hadn't met Karim. Going to places where there were no familiar faces, where no one was expecting him, had become a regular occurrence for him. Since the disastrous casting, he could no longer stand seeing his friends, who all unintentionally reminded him of his past. So Martin accompanied his friend to the apartment of the young unknown couple, these two examples of normality.

Karim brought some strong alcohol, planning to get drunk more quickly. Martin brought a single bottle of Schweppes. They remained off to the side at the start, stuck at the back of the kitchen. Karim got drunk and wanted to go and dance in the living room. Martin joined in a few random conversations, throwing in the odd comment here and there, as if his thoughts could be scattered to the winds. It's hard to know at what point in the evening he and Sophie moved closer to one another. There comes a time of night when time no longer exists. Whenever she came to grab a beer from the fridge, she saw him there, like a beacon in the middle of the party. In the end she went to speak to him, but since Martin wasn't too adept at conversation, it quickly turned into a monologue. Do we open up more easily when met with silence? Sophie certainly did. She told Martin that she was in the middle of finishing her studies in medicine and was preparing for her first job. As a child, she had loved playing doctor and patient with her brother. At four or five years old, she had listened to his chest with her plastic instruments, delivered improbable diagnoses and made him drink concoctions that she deemed miracle cures. Subjected to this imaginary medical care, her brother never fell ill. Sophie saw it as a clear sign of her gift. There is something wonderful about the idea that a child's game can become an adult's occupation – that's what she told him. But deep down, she had only one wish: to know more about her silent interlocutor. Who was he?

Martin had loved listening to the words of this unknown girl who had opened up to him so easily. He was so focused on every detail of her account that he was no longer paying attention to the other guests, who were shoving past him to get a drink or to tap their ash out of the window. Listening to this girl talk was like extricating himself from the crowd. He instinctively felt comfortable with her, which was extremely rare for Martin, who got excited about as often as it rains in Ethiopia. Now it was his turn to talk. Sophie had asked, 'What about you? What do you do?' You always had to define yourself, have things to say about yourself, offer up your past in exchange for the present. He dreamed of an encounter that wasn't based on anything concrete like that. It reminded him of Flaubert's words to Louise Colet: 'What seems beautiful to me, what I should like to write, is a book about nothing, a book dependent on nothing external, which would be held together by the strength of its style.' Yes, that was exactly his desire: to meet someone he didn't have to explain himself to. To have an encounter held together by the strength of its style.

He was rescued from the anticipated confession by the return of Karim, who was by now completely drunk. 'Where were you? I've been looking for you everywhere!' – a completely improbable statement in a two-bedroom apartment. His arrival was nothing more than a very short diversion. He disappeared immediately, and Martin didn't see him again that evening. But it gave him the opportunity to explain: 'We're colleagues at the Louvre.' These few words seemed to appeal to Sophie. Mentioning a prestigious museum during a romantic job interview was impressively effective. Martin launched into an explanation of his career path, but the longer he spoke, the quieter his voice became. Unconvinced by what he was saying, Martin could hear that his tale had taken on the feel of a self-help book written by Schopenhauer. Sophie found him truly unusual, which only increased his appeal. But every time she wanted to know more, he eluded her. He was like a man trying to escape his own biographer.

Martin suddenly thought about Mathilde, and their conversations in the evening; the beauty of those moments when they were getting to know one another. And then he thought about how he had ruined that relationship. He needed to draw strength from his shame, the strength to be a different man. Which is exactly what he did. Changing his tone completely, he began to talk. Sophie had the feeling she was listening to a man in the process of changing his trajectory, like an aeroplane altering course. He was changing his destination. Now his sentences ran on with ease, as he passed from a theory about clouds to David Lynch's early films. Sophie had never met anyone so unusual, so funny. She didn't even notice the night passing until daylight appeared. They left the party together, but neither of them seemed to understand the other's wishes. Sophie waited for Martin to make the first move, without knowing that in matters of love he had only ever hovered around the edges. At a time when romance was often all about immediacy, there was perhaps a certain charm in leaving these two – illiterate in matters of the heart – to get on with it. They exchanged phone numbers and said goodbye. Once they were both home, they each realised that they'd been stupid. Before falling asleep, Sophie thought about how she'd felt a few hours earlier. She hadn't wanted to go to the party, but one of her friends had insisted. Wasn't that always the way? The most important encounters happen despite our intentions. With that in mind, we should always do the opposite of what we intend. As for Martin, it was only once he was already in bed that he realised: I met her in a kitchen!

26

A few days later, they met for lunch. Martin didn't want to tell his whole life story on their first date. He knew he would reveal everything to her, but for the time being, he loved the innocence of the look Sophie gave him. Meeting someone new means we can start afresh, without our past. We tell them what we want to; we can skip pages, or even start at the end. This newfound narrative freedom ended with Sophie inviting him to dinner. Martin agonised over which flowers to bring, before finally asking the florist for 'one of each'. This bizarre bouquet turned out to be strangely harmonious. Sophie thanked her guest and put the flowers in a vase. Martin entered a charming little living room. Over the sofa he saw a poster for John Cassavetes's *Opening Night*. Sophie suggested they sit down for an aperitif, but Martin signalled to her to wait. He headed to a small bookshelf on the other side of the room. Had she met some kind of literary psychopath? The moment he arrived at her place he had begun meticulously examining her books. Eventually, she asked him:

'Can I help you? Is there something in particular you're searching for?'

'Sorry, I'm just looking . . .'

'Is this your bottom line? You'll only stay for dinner if you like my books?' she asked, to lighten the mood, bothered by this situation she didn't understand.

After a moment, Martin turned around with a huge smile. No *Harry Potter*.

PART FOUR

1

Martin's intuition had been correct: only love could put an end to his suffering. Sophie had given him back his self-confidence. He felt capable of taking responsibility for his failure, rather than suffering because of it. Now that he was loved, he was no longer vulnerable. It was sweet, and almost miraculous. When Harry Potter loomed, all he had to do was look away. The whole tragic story seemed to be over.

2

Martin was still working at the Louvre, and Sophie had set up in her practice. When Martin had a stomach ache, he went to Sophie; when Sophie wanted to soothe her soul, she went to see Martin. They took long walks in the Jardin des Tuileries with their dog, Jack. At the start of their relationship, there was a moment that confirmed they were destined for one another. While they were shopping for their dinner, Sophie had said to Martin: 'Don't forget to get those yoghurts you like.' It was exactly what his father had said before he collapsed, the last sentence of their normal life. Martin froze for a second, looking at Sophie as though she were a crack in reality. In the end, he felt this incredible coincidence was a sign from his father; a sort of blessing from beyond the grave.

Jeanne had recently married Nicolas, a police inspector she had met three years earlier under rather unusual circumstances. At the time, Marc had been trying to re-establish contact with her. While reading *Le Point*, he gathered that she had returned to France. Since then, he had taken to waiting outside her office every night. She had agreed to speak to him. He swore he had changed, and claimed that he wanted to apologise to Martin. He presented himself as a new man – sincere, and ashamed of his behaviour in the past. But Jeanne remained on her guard, fearing more than anything that she would fall once again for his manipulative tricks. In reaction to the distance she was keeping between them, he became more and more aggressive. Jeanne had no choice but to report him for harassment. And so it was that during her trip to the police station, as she tried in vain to get a coffee from the uncooperative machine, Nicolas had come to her aid. Life has a funny way of working out.

As for Karim, he was still very much a part of Martin's life. His fate had been an interesting one. A few weeks after the party where Martin had met Sophie, Karim received a call from Jacques Audiard. He hesitated at first (the fear of relapse), but curiosity got the better of him. So he found himself once again facing the great director, who seemed genuinely happy to see the actor who had almost been his *Prophet*. Audiard quickly explained to Karim that he pictured him in one of the roles in his new project, *Rust and Bone*, as a colleague of Marion Cotillard's. The action would take place in an aquarium, alongside dolphins and sea lions. To prepare for the role he would have to join a team of real animal trainers. It was hard to imagine a bigger lure for a young actor. But Karim said right away that he needed to think about it. Audiard tried to keep the stupefied expression from his face – it had been years since he'd had an actor not immediately accept one of his proposals. Karim explained that he had stopped acting after the casting for *A Prophet*. Audiard tried to reason with him. It was crazy for someone with his talent to give up. He thought of that phrase so often heard in situations like this: 'You have to get back on the horse.' He even tried to add a humorous spin: 'Don't get back on the horse, get on a dolphin instead.' Karim smiled, but his mind was elsewhere. He was thinking of the happiness this conversation would have brought him a few years earlier. But it was no longer possible. He had suffered too much – far too much. So he stood up, insisted on paying for the coffees, and then calmly announced: 'Monsieur Audiard, I sincerely thank you for the offer, but the answer is no.' And he left.

That evening, he told Martin everything. Though what his friend had achieved didn't change Martin's own story, it did at least reassure him. The distressing thing about failure is losing control of your destiny, submitting to someone else's decision. In acting this way, Karim hadn't fixed anything – but he felt as though he had taken back control. It was he who would decide his own destiny, and this act of bravery moved Martin. Through his actions, Karim had avenged the honour of all the second bests.

3

There are certain kinds of pain that seem insurmountable. After these years of respite, Martin felt himself overwhelmed once more by his failure. Lethargy is always one of the first signs of melancholy. He began to do everything more slowly: getting up, washing, eating, thinking. Sophie didn't know what to do – she had never experienced Martin's dark periods before. He was wallowing once more in his bitterness, and went out less and less. He asked himself constantly, 'Why has this come back? Why?' It was incomprehensible. He started to avoid watching television again, for fear of coming across a *Harry Potter* film. The troubles of his past had returned without warning.

Sophie sought help from Jeanne, who was distraught when she heard of her son's relapse. She remembered all the tactics they had tried over the years. But nothing had really worked until the day Martin had found love. Which is why Jeanne felt she could ask:

'Is everything okay between you two?'

'Why would you ask me that? Of course. I love him more than anything. And it kills me to see him like this.'

'. . .'

'I want so much to help him. To find a solution.'

Indeed, Sophie thought about Martin constantly. As a doctor, she tried to rationalise the situation.

'Darling, there must have been a trigger. You don't just relapse like that.'

'I don't know.'

'Stress at work? Fear of another failure?'

No, it wasn't that. In fact, they were giving him more responsibilities at the Louvre. He trawled through his recent memories but found nothing. He retraced every detail, but nothing came to mind – he hadn't even seen anyone reading a J. K. Rowling book on the Métro. Martin felt hopeless. It was all coming back to him. His attempts to avoid the life of the Other, the desire to cut himself off from the world, the superhuman efforts simply to buy a book or go to the cinema – yes, it was all coming back. Why? He and Sophie made a wonderful couple, so what was it? Was he condemned to unhappiness no matter what?

4

A few weeks earlier, the couple had discussed the possibility of having a child. They had even thought of a name: Sacha if it was a boy, and Sasha if it was a girl. It was this discussion that had been the source of Martin's relapse. In projecting himself into his future as a father, he had sunk back into the world of his childhood. He pictured his child watching or reading *Harry Potter*. Years had passed, and the phenomenon hadn't faded. They had even built theme parks dedicated to the wizard in Orlando and Osaka in Japan. Having a child would surely mean confronting that universe once more. It was like saying to a recovering drug addict: 'You're going to fill a huge bowl with cocaine and carry it around with you at all times.' That might seem like an extreme comparison – but becoming a father when you have issues with Harry Potter was bound to put you in an uncomfortable situation.

The worst consequence of a failure is that it transforms the rest of your life into a perpetual failure. Martin knew he would never overcome it. One thing was certain: he didn't want to inflict his profound frailty on his future children – and even less on the woman he loved. So he told Sophie that they should break up. Sophie protested.

'Darling, I can see you're suffering. But please don't be ridiculous. We aren't going to break up. We're going to fight this together.'

'I don't want to be a burden to you.'

'You never will be.'

'I can't do this any more. It's haunted me for two decades.'

'I know. But you've been doing so well the last few years. There's no reason you can't find that happiness again.'

'I want to be done with it for good. I've tried to reason with myself: you didn't get the role, so what? But I can't.'

'I understand, darling. But you are thirty years old, and you have everything going for you. You are not going to let this ruin your life. Our life.'

'. . .'

'I promise you we'll figure it out.'

5

Sophie began to do some research. She came across some articles on conferences about failure, dubbed 'FailCons'. Launched in the USA, they had now spread across the world. Large events were organised near and far, in which participants recounted stories of all their failures. During a well-attended rally in 2015, *L'Express* had run a headline that said: ALL THE LOSERS REUNITE IN TOULOUSE. English speakers will easily see that even the choice of the host city had formed an integral part of the project. There were slogans such as FAILURE IS PART OF SUCCESS! but it was mainly about listening to inspiring life stories. There were entrepreneurs who had gone bankrupt, artists coming out of a dry spell, even members of the Socialist Party. Sophie showed these videos to Martin. They reminded him of his long-ago session with Dr Xenakis. For Martin, listening to the failures of others in order to feel better about yourself – it was old hat.

6

So Sophie began to consider all kinds of medical and paramedical practices, from osteopathy to etiopathy, sophrology to acupuncture. She quickly realised that Martin wouldn't want to see anyone. He was ill at ease with the idea of sharing his angst, even during silent sessions. She eventually thought of the power of writing. It is often said that words can soothe pain. It was the same with painting, or any other form of artistic expression, through what is broadly called art therapy. But Martin felt the greatest affinity with writing.

He had already scribbled a few pages over the years, in a sort of intimate journal, or thought diary. And then he had thrown them all away, not wanting to hold on to any trace of his confessions. Sophie encouraged him to begin writing a new story of his life. To finally explain what he had been through, in a controlled manner. Why not? he thought. He would write it for himself, like someone packing their suitcase without going on holiday. To distance himself from it, he decided to write his story in the third person. The first few days brought him respite. When he returned home from the Louvre, he sat at his desk. Sophie arranged to go out in the evenings to see friends, to give Martin some peace and quiet. When she was at home, she shut herself away in their bedroom. From time to time, she would approach Martin to check everything was all right, and he would immediately shoo her away. He seemed to be concentrating intensely. To help summon the memories of his childhood, he had lunch with his mother and asked her questions about it. He had completely forgotten that she had met his father at a Cure concert. For Jeanne, it seemed so long ago. The music of her youth wasn't even played on the radio any more.

One Saturday afternoon, about a month after the beginning of this literary enterprise, Sophie went over to the manuscript. Martin had printed out the first few pages, finding it more practical for re-reading. Which was how Sophie discovered the title: *How I Ruined My Life*. Not only did she find it rather off-putting, she also couldn't understand why he would write such a statement. It was absurd, given what he had accomplished, and, furthermore, not very gratifying in terms of their love story. When he returned to the room, she said, a little coldly:

'I saw your title.'

'. . .'

'A bit depressing, isn't it? I mean, it wouldn't make me want to read your book.'

'. . .'

'I honestly thought writing would do you good, but you've gone and chosen such a gloomy title . . . and thanks a lot, by the way.'

'. . .'

'What do you want me to say to you? If you've "ruined your life"?'

Sophie left the living room and hid away in the bedroom. Martin had not anticipated this at all. The title was based on his overriding feeling: that of a failure so overwhelming that, no matter what you did, it would dictate the course of your life. Of course he didn't mean it about Sophie. He had been intending to write about how much her love had helped him. Had saved him, even.

Feeling foolish, he went to the bedroom. He knelt beside the bed and stammered:

'Forgive me. The title wasn't about you at all. On the contrary – you're the most wonderful thing that has ever happened to me. You know that . . .'

'. . .'

'Darling, please.' At that moment, Sophie turned around and took Martin's hand. He said a few more words in apology, before continuing: 'I'm going to stop writing. You were right, at the beginning it did me good. I felt like I was organising things in my head. But now I'm coming up to the audition . . . and I don't want to inflict that on myself. To talk about everything that hurt me again.'

'I understand.'

'I'm so scared you think I'm too much. There must be times when you feel I'm exaggerating.'

'No. I feel your pain, I really do. And I think it's justified. It just hurts to not be able to help you.'

'. . .'

'I'm always trying to find the right words to make you feel better. You know, I'm not comparing it to what you've been through, but I think it's symptomatic of our time.'

'What do you mean?'

'When I go on Instagram and see other people's amazing lives, I also feel like my life is nothing, or that it's wasted.'

'. . .'

'These days we live under the tyranny of other people's happiness. Or their supposed happiness, in any case.'

Martin's mind lingered on that expression, 'the tyranny of other people's happiness'. That would have made a good title. But he'd made his decision – he would abandon his writing project. He understood now that words could free you from what was buried deep within, and had even started to feel it himself – a kind of therapy through commas. But in the end, it wasn't for him. By going in search of the vestiges of his suffering, he felt as though it was growing once more. And so he had to start again from scratch, in utter uncertainty.

7

There were arguments and reconciliations; there were fears for the future and refuge in the beauty of the past. The couple who had everything they needed to live a peaceful life were in the process of becoming belligerent with each other. Martin had ruined his life because he would rather suffer alone. He had tried everything, and nothing had worked.

And it was then.

It was then that one evening Sophie went to Martin. Close to him, far too close. Her expression seemed different; even the way she had turned the key in the lock had seemed new. Martin lifted his head in her direction, attempted a smile; but displays of affection required an inordinate effort. His love for Sophie couldn't outweigh the disdain he felt for himself. With her mouth pressed to his ear, she whispered: 'I think I've found the solution.'

8

Martin questioned her, but she wouldn't reveal anything. The next evening, she simply asked him to dress to go out. Nothing extravagant, just a shirt and jacket. She was taking him . . . somewhere. He hated surprises; usually he planned his every move for fear of confronting the unexpected. She promised they weren't going far; it was ten minutes by foot at most to reach their destination.

Outside, the atmosphere was strangely calm. The city seemed to be holding its breath, as though it too were waiting to see what would happen. They arrived outside the Ritz, the hotel at the Place Vendôme. Instinctively, Martin thought that Sophie had organised one of those romantic evenings intended to bring a couple closer together: a candlelit dinner in a gorgeous setting. Beauty would always remain a recourse in the face of uncertainty. But apparently not. Sophie announced:

'Here's where we go our separate ways.'

'. . .'

There was a playful tone to her words. Martin would have to enter the hotel alone, without knowing what was going to happen. His heart was beating fast, as though it wanted to escape from his body. This was all going in an uncomfortable direction. All he wanted to do was turn around and go home. But he had no choice. The look Sophie gave him was not a suggestion: it was an order.

Before leaving him, she added simply: 'Go to the Bar Hemingway.' He entered the hotel, where a sign pointed to the bar, down a long corridor with a red carpet. After an almost deserted Paris, Martin met nobody here either. It accentuated the feeling that this moment was happening outside reality. The bar was there, in front of him. He took the time to read a small notice, which proclaimed that the great American writer had drunk fifty-one dry Martinis here to celebrate the liberation of Paris. This liquid posterity was certainly amusing, but he wasn't in the mood to ponder it. He wanted to know; he wanted to understand.

Martin entered the bar very slowly, as though afraid of waking it up. The waiter lifted his head, but made no particular move towards him, continuing to arrange his bottles meticulously. The room was oddly empty; no businessmen or illicit couples. There was just one person sitting at the bar, with a cocktail in front of him that Martin couldn't identify. Martin was instinctively heading for one of the chairs when the sole customer turned towards him.

It was Daniel Radcliffe.

9

The night before, Sophie had learned that the actor was returning to Paris for Claire Denis's new film. Just like Robert Pattinson, Daniel Radcliffe had said in an interview that he dreamed of working with the director. So she and Christine Angot had written a screenplay for him. *Milk City* told the story of a young Englishman roaming the streets of a hostile Paris. Radcliffe felt comfortable in this atmosphere, light years away from *Harry Potter*.

Sophie loved getting her patients to talk; there was surely a frustrated psychologist lying dormant within her. As the young woman she'd been giving a routine check-up got dressed, Sophie asked: 'And what are you up to at the moment?'

A contract worker in the entertainment industry, the woman replied: 'Not much . . . Just some odd jobs as an extra. Yesterday I was in a Claire Denis film, with Daniel Radcliffe.'

Sophie dropped the pen she was holding. She cancelled the rest of the day's appointments, and literally ran to the address her patient had given her. Luckily, they were still shooting. After filming the exterior shots in the street, the team had taken over a small building in the eleventh arrondissement for the scenes set in the main character's apartment. There were two bodyguards preventing access to the set, which was rare for a low-budget film – Daniel Radcliffe's fans had been camped out all day trying to get a glimpse of their idol. Sophie realised it would be difficult to get in touch with the star. They would think she was a groupie too. After a while, she caught sight of a girl on the team whose job it was to stop cars coming down the street, presumably to avoid too much noise during takes. Taking advantage of the moment of calm, Sophie approached her. 'If I give you a letter for Daniel Radcliffe, do you think you could pass it on to him?' The girl replied kindly, 'I can give it to him, sure, but I can't promise he'll read it.'

So Sophie sat in a nearby café, and began to write the letter in English. Just a few simple words – it needed to be succinct. She knew the actor must be inundated with requests. On the envelope, she wrote FROM MARTIN HILL. THE OTHER POTTER – in large letters to attract his attention. The girl kept her promise and put the letter in the actor's dressing room. Two hours later, Sophie thought she might faint – the actor had sent her a text.

10

And so they met for the first time. Martin was stunned, and ordered a glass of wine to calm his nerves. But Daniel welcomed him with a huge smile; clearly, he wanted to put him at ease. For twenty years, no one had ever acted completely normally around him. But today, he too was nervous. Opposite him was the life he might have had.

Martin hadn't spoken English for a long time; after the series of tragic events, it had become a dead language to him. On top of the shock and the stress of this meeting, he had to search for the vocabulary of his childhood. Thankfully, Daniel took control of the conversation.

'You know, I've often thought about you. At the time, when I got the role, I was ecstatic, but I knew very well that there were two of us in the final round. I even wanted to call you, but I didn't. I was afraid of saying something trite, or that you would be angry with me.'

'. . .'

'And yet, no one could understand you better than me. I remember the awful wait for the verdict. I told myself so many times that it wasn't going to be me. I imagined that everything would end there.'

'But it didn't.'

'No. You know, I remember asking the producer if I could see your audition.'

'Really? Why?'

'I don't know. Maybe to understand why they chose me. I knew they had gone back and forth between us, so I wanted to see what made the difference.'

'I never saw the tape.'

'Nor did I in the end.'

'When I did the audition, everyone seemed so excited,' Martin explained, his confidence bolstered by Daniel's sincerity. 'That was the hardest part. I'd have preferred it if they'd told me right away that I was rubbish, instead of going through all that . . .'

'I know. I know . . . but I think you *were* their first choice, for a long time. And then they changed their minds.'

The conversation flowed naturally. They were two sides of the same coin, and it brought them together. In the end they ordered a bottle of red wine and settled in the semi-darkness at the back of the bar. A couple sat down a little way away without spotting Daniel. If they had, they would have immediately asked for a photo. 'Even people who don't care about me or Harry Potter at all still want a selfie, just to show it to everyone. One day I actually tried to count the number of pictures I must be in: surely more than a million. In twenty years, I must have broken the record for the most time spent smiling,' Daniel added, before returning to the subject of the audition.

'At the beginning, when I thought about you, I felt sad. Or maybe I even felt pity. I mean . . . I was imagining how hard that must have been.'

'. . .'

'It was so strange. I really thought a lot about the injustice of it. And then I realised why.'

'Why?'

'I was moving at this . . . extravagant, crazy, exhausting pace. When I thought about you, it was to wonder what my life would have been like without Harry Potter. I quickly realised it was over for me. I would never have a normal life again.'

'. . .'

'And . . .'

'What?'

'Maybe you'll think this is strange . . . but sometimes it was so hard. So I think I envied you. No, really – I told myself my life would have been better without all this. This was when I was stressed, or tired, of course, but in any case, it was you I thought about. It became almost an obsession.'

Martin was stunned. He had suffered so much from having an extraordinary existence pass him by, and now here was Daniel Radcliffe expressing the same sort of regret. Although Martin didn't know it yet, this simple notion would allow him to even the score a bit. There was no longer a winner or a loser. Of course, Daniel only felt these things at difficult moments – but he felt them nonetheless.

'I know I've had some incredible experiences. But it was at the expense of everything else,' Daniel said.

'. . .'

'Right from the start, nothing was ever the same again. In my neighbourhood, everyone wanted to be my best friend. My old classmates even fought over it. It became unbearable. Nothing was real any more. I wasn't Daniel, I was Harry.'

'. . .'

'And others had it even worse. Tom, who plays Draco Malfoy, the villain . . . other kids would spit at him in the street. They couldn't tell the difference between the films and reality. I was reading about his mental health struggles a few months ago. It upset me . . . but I also understood it.'

'. . .'

'Anyway, we were shut away more and more. There was a school just for us, with a special timetable. The rest of the time, we were filming. We were condemned to living together.'

'In a few articles I read, it sounded amazing.'

'Of course, we were a real group of friends. But I couldn't do anything else. I couldn't go to the cinema, or walk down the street. I'm not complaining, but I'm just telling you that that life . . . sometimes it was very hard.'

'. . .'

'No one behaved normally around me any more. Once I read an anecdote that Ringo Starr told, where he described exactly that.'

'What did he say?'

'He was at his aunt's house, and he dropped his cup of tea.'

'And?'

'Everyone rushed to pick it up. When before he would have got a smack. It's scary, honestly.'

'You know, Daniel, I can see where you're going with this, and it really is kind of you. You're trying to take away some of my resentment. And it's true, it does make me feel better to hear what you've said . . .'

'I'm not trying to make amends for getting the role. I know very well it's not my fault. You think my life has been brilliant. Besides, I do love being an actor. Honestly, I don't even think I'm saying all this just for you. These are things that have weighed heavily on me too, and it's a relief to talk about them. You think I don't know that Harry Potter has no right to complain? Yes, my life is great. Yes, the whole world dreams of being in my place. But I . . . there are times I would give anything to not be myself, just for a day.'

'. . .'

'Daily life was often hell. There were hours of make-up. And I couldn't go skiing, or sit in the sun. Sure, when you say it like that – who cares? But when someone takes away your freedom, you'll see how these things become obsessions.'

'. . .'

'There was a time when I couldn't take it any more. I almost packed it all in. It's common knowledge that I had some problems with alcohol. In any case, as soon as things started going badly, the whole world knew about it. If I pissed the wrong way, it was on the front page of the *Daily Mail* the next day. I'm constantly hounded. Does that sound fun to you?'

'No, I don't think it does.'

'Even my dogs have bodyguards, can you imagine?'

'No.'

'I mean, they have fans too . . . they get plenty of presents. Can you believe this crazy world?'

'. . .'

'When Harry Potter finished, I told myself I would finally be able to breathe. Get some air. I got a part in a play. And it was just awful. There were hordes of photographers every night. I just wanted to act. After a while, I had an idea. I wore the same clothes every day. It meant the paparazzi photos were less valuable, you know, they couldn't put a date on them . . . They couldn't sell the same photo over and over again.'

'. . .'

'And I can't begin to tell you all the ridiculous things I've read about myself. I just found out that supposedly I ordered a statue in my own likeness! I don't know where that came from. Especially since I'm so sick of seeing my own face! It's utter nonsense.'

Clearly, Daniel needed to talk. Listening to him, you'd think he could have written *How I Ruined My Life* himself. His story was certainly extreme, but it allowed Martin to see things in a new light. What was success, really? What was failure? His frustration had come from the fantasy of another life that he'd thought was better. But what did he really know about the everyday life of the Other? Not much, beyond what the media said.

Daniel continued his melancholic litany, but this time with a hint of humour and self-mockery.

'And even worse – no one knows my name!'

'. . .'

'On the street, everyone calls me Harry! Harry this, Harry that! All day long I hear, "Oh, it's Harry! Come on, let's ask Harry for a photo!" And it will be like that for the rest of my life. I mean, I'm in the process of making a film right now, and nobody cares. Or they'll say, "Ah, it's got the guy who played Harry Potter in it!" As hard as I work, as much as I motivate myself, I'll always be stuck in that role. So yes – it's wonderful. But it's a gilded cage.'

'. . .'

'You'll think I'm exaggerating, but sometimes I feel I sold my youth to the devil.'

Daniel stopped there, before adding how happy he was to have met Martin. Now he wanted to know more about him. What had he been doing all these years? 'Me? Not much . . .' was all Martin said at first. And then he started again. No, that wasn't true. He had a career that he loved, and a wonderful partner. A partner to whom he owed this life-changing moment. Although he had relapsed recently, he could talk about the last years of his life with happiness. He still described the difficult times, the need to hide himself away permanently, and the strange feeling that his life resembled Harry Potter's. His story went on for a long time, and he left nothing out – from the difficulty he had buying a book, up to his trip to Polish Hogwarts. Daniel was overwhelmed. This story could have been his. He felt a huge amount of empathy for Martin. It is rare that someone has access to their alternative reality. Our unique trajectory doesn't give us the slightest glimpse of the paths we didn't take.

In a way, they had both dreamed of having the other one's life. Each longed for what he didn't have. One wanted the light, the other the shadows. In meeting one another, Daniel and Martin both felt soothed. And in a way, they had filled in the gaps in their destiny. But it wouldn't end there. Not only had they decided to meet again, but also that they would each truly experience the other one's life. Daniel would take Martin to a Golden Globe Awards ceremony, and Martin invited Daniel to spend a whole day in a room at the Louvre. People never looked at museum attendants. In uniform, no one would recognise him. No one would imagine that the man who said, 'No flash, please,' was none other than Harry Potter.

The evening of their first meeting, just before leaving, Daniel asked Martin, 'Is there anything I can do for you?'

Martin thought about it for a moment, then said: 'Yes.'[9]

---

9 A few months later, during an advance screening, Daniel Radcliffe would wear an umbrella-tie. Exciting first curiosity and then enthusiasm, this accessory would become a roaring success.

11

It was very late when Martin returned home, walking through the Parisian night. For the first time in a long time, he felt light. He felt as though he had rediscovered the child he had once been – the child from before the audition. But above all, he thought about Sophie. She had been incredible. He never would have imagined that meeting Daniel would have made him feel so much better. On the contrary, he had spent his life avoiding him, envying him, hating him. Martin finally understood the value of not having been chosen.

He opened the door to his apartment, taking care not to make any noise. In the living room, the abandoned manuscript caught his eye. Maybe he would pick it up again. In the bedroom, Sophie was sleeping peacefully. He stood motionless for a moment, watching her in the darkness, spellbound by her shoulder where it emerged from beneath the sheet. His life could begin.

Also available from Gallic Books by David Foenkinos

THE MARTINS

TRANSLATED BY SAM TAYLOR

'Go out into the street and the first person you see will be the subject of your next book.'

This is the challenge a struggling Parisian writer sets himself, imagining his next heroine might be the mysterious young woman who often stands smoking near his apartment . . . instead it's octogenarian Madeleine. She's happy to become the subject of his book – but first she needs to put away her shopping.

Is it really true, the writer wonders, that every life is the stuff of novels, or is his story doomed to be hopelessly banal? As he gets to know Madeleine and her family, he'll be privy to their secrets: lost loves, marital problems and workplace worries. And he'll soon realise he is not the impartial bystander he intended to be, but a catalyst for major changes in the lives of his characters.

Told with Foenkinos's characteristic irony and self-deprecating humour, yet filled with warmth, *The Martins* is a compelling tale of the family next door which raises questions about what it means to be 'ordinary', and about the blurred lines between truth and fiction.

PAPERBACK 9781913547301

EBOOK 9781913547349